An Island Sanctuary

An Island Sanctuary

S V Diggle

Blenheim Press Limited
Codicote

Published in 2009
by
Blenheim Press Ltd
Codicote Innovation Centre
St Albans Road
Codicote
Herts SG4 8WH

ISBN 978-1-906302-14-6

Typeset by TW Typesetting, Plymouth, Devon

Printed and bound in Great Britain by
CPI Antony Rowe, Chippenham and Eastbourne

*I dedicate this book to my son Jonathan
who accompanied me on my first visit
to Holy Island and subsequent visits,
and
to my daughter Hilary Girling for her support.*

LIVING BY THE SEA WITH ITS VAST HUGE SKIES
YOU SEE NATURE IN ALL ITS MOODS
YESTERDAY HAD BEEN UNKIND
WHEN I LOOKED OUT OF THE WINDOW
A MIST-LIKE DRIZZLE PREVAILED ALL DAY
A COLD WIND NIPPED THE END OF YOUR NOSE & LOBES OF YOUR EARS
BUT TO-DAY THE SUN CAME OUT IN A CLOUDLESS SKY
AS I WALK ACROSS THE FIELD IN SIGHT OF THE SEA
TOWARDS THE CASTLE ON THE ROCK
BRIGHT, PEACEFUL & HAZY WITH A TRAIL OF SMOKE
ON THE HORIZON FROM A PASSING SHIP
THE AIR BEAT IN FROM THE SEA, FRESH-AIR, STRONG & SALTY

ONE

A strong wind was blowing the morning Bert Watts started out for a day's fishing. Dark clouds were gathering in the south west, trees bent under the strain, wooden fences rocked furiously, leaves and paper spun around in circles before being lifted and carried away. As he drew nearer to the harbour he could see the boats moored along the quayside heaving on their mooring ropes as the sea, now whipped by the increasing force, climbed up the harbour wall.

Bert Watts had fished all his life for a living. He was born on the Island of Lindisfarne three miles off the Northumberland coast. During the Second World War he had joined the Merchant Navy and was torpedoed twice, on the second occasion being rescued by a British frigate after spending two days in an open boat. After the war he married Mary Pickering, a local girl, who gave him a son, Robert.

Bringing his pick-up truck to a halt at the harbour, he braced himself against the invisible force slamming the truck door behind him. It was 6.30 am on this October morning in 1987. Turning the collar of his anorak up around his cheeks he set off towards his boat the *Northern Pride*, a twenty-foot clinker-built boat moored astern five other boats along the quayside. He was not the only early riser that morning. Alf Everitt, a near neighbour, was already on the quay taking his early morning walk. Like Bert, Alf had lived on the island all his life, as a farmer, marrying Sally Price the daughter of the landlord of the local pub. Sally had been taken away from him two years ago in a most unusual tragic manner. She had just washed the kitchen floor when she slipped and fell, hitting her head against the corner of the Aga cooker. She died in hospital, never regaining consciousness. Alf had never really got over it, and spent most of his days just walking around the island.

'Morning Bert,' Alf greeted him as he got closer.

'Eh, 'morning Alf. Bit fresh today.'

'Look at them clouds,' Alf said pointing upwards. 'They're going at a fair rate Bert, and look over there how black they are.'

'Certainly are Alf, it'll blow the cobwebs away.'

'You mind it don't blow you away, Bert.'

'I've been out in worse, I'll be back by 10, just going to put a few pots out.'

' I wouldn't go out just yet, Bert. Can't you wait a bit?'

'Got to earn a living, not all like you retired.'

Alf stood and watched him descend the iron ladder fixed to the quay wall leading to his boat. Bert got busy attending to the boat's engine. After a few moments it sprang into life, sending up a cloud of smoke. Bert rubbed his hands on a piece of cloth which he produced from his pocket then set about casting off the mooring ropes. Alf watched him coil the ropes on deck amongst the many crab pots stacked neatly along the bulwarks.

'Rather you than me, Bert,' Alf shouted above the noise of the engine.

'Got to bring the bacon home Alf!' he laughed.

Alf threw the last remaining mooring rope down to him.

'Ta,' shouted Bert, and increasing the engine speed drew slowly away from the quayside, turning the boat gradually round to face the open sea, then waved his hand as the boat lurched forward. Alf stood and watched him as the boat entered the open sea beyond the harbour entrance. He shook his head as he watched it being tossed about, then turned and walked slowly back home.

Alf and his late wife were the two oldest inhabitants on the Island. Before he married Sally, she lived at home in the pub with her parents and sister Doreen. One day during the War she had witnessed a German fighter plane shot down during the daylight hours. The terrified pilot was brought to the pub that day to wait until the military arrived.

Once outside the harbour Bert's boat was lifted and tilted like a child's toy boat. The sea in front of him was like molten steel heaving and churning as the boat ploughed through the waves. The sky was now a faint steelish blue with seagulls screaming as they were caught in the strong wind and carried away at a fast rate.

The boat was about three quarters of a mile out to sea when Bert Watts cut the engine. With no propulsion the boat was lifted high on the crest of the waves before being slammed down again into the trough. Bert Watts was not unduly worried; he had encountered weather like this before when the sea was very angry. He had a job to do.

He was engrossed preparing his crab pots to a depth of six fathoms, putting about thirty pots on each shank, cursing the seals inwardly for stealing the bait with their long slender necks. Today he thought the rough sea would bring his catch further inland, oblivious that a change in the visibility was taking place behind him. Thick banks of storm clouds were building up in the east. A frightening change was taking place. Northern and eastern horizons were closing in with dark purple-coloured clouds. In the far distance a thin band of dancing silver spread along the horizon. The boat began to heave more as the height of the driven sea was forced even higher. Within minutes the silver band had grown into a huge menacing wave over seventy feet high and was racing towards the shore at an incredible rate. The *Northern Pride* was lifted high like a box of matches, as Bert worked frantically with the pots, lowering them over the side of the boat.

Realising he was now in a danger zone, he started the engine, only to have it die on him. The sea had now swamped his deck, and ropes and crab pots began to swill about the deck. He was now at the mercy of the restless heaving sea. Again he tried to get the engine to fire. It spluttered then died.

'Come on old girl, let's get home,' he said to the engine. Bert's attempt failed again. 'Shit!'

Again it spluttered, coughed and remained silent. He was working hard now, every second was vital.

'Come on you bloody swine – FIRE!' Then with a big bang and a cloud of smoke it sprang into action. 'Good girl, now let's get out of here.'

The sea was now a uniform black mass, bleak and angry. Behind were further great waves of tumultuous foaming heavy water getting closer. The boat's engines were working hard against this mountainous, incessant battering. One moment it was in a deep trough of water, the next it was held high with its propellers turning in the air. But still it battled on, being lifted then smashed down at will. The clouds appeared lower, as if right on top of them, large ominous black/purple clouds bearing down on this puny insignificant boat which offered no contest to them as they brought all their strength and might to it. By now the deck was awash, almost submerged. Bert was encountering one of the worst storms of his life. The boat began to descend into a deep cauldron of seething, boiling sea. The deck now completely awash, the boat sat lower in the water, its bows rising sharply, knocking the helm from Bert's grasp.

3

Then it happened. The boat's engine, now completely swamped, spluttered and died. Now there was just the sound of the raging wind and the turbulent sea. Bert knew the outcome. He was doomed. With no power he had lost control of the boat and his battle with the sea. He was about to lose his life. The *Northern Pride* had given up its fight for survival and awaited its fate. It was now only a matter of time.

Then it came – the sea broke, bringing all its might and strength in a single sheet of water crashing down on the small boat, drenching the deck and sweeping overboard crab pots, ropes and everything in its fury. It came in with all its might and with one great enormous wave lifted the boat high as if offering it to the Gods, turned it over and brought it down with such force it broke the boat into two pieces. Halfway down, the high wave hovering above suddenly broke and crashed down, smashing the now exhausted and broken boat into the dark heaving sea. Pitched into darkness beneath a wall of water Bert tried desperately and helplessly to cling to life. The great wall of water sat poised for a moment before delivering the death blow. It came sweeping down onto him, his last moments on this earth were nearly over. Lifted high like a rag doll he soon became a victim of a violent sea as his strength ebbed from him and finally gave out.

Mary Watts was working in her kitchen preparing a hot meal ready for Bert's return. She was aware of the strong wind buffeting the windows, and occasionally the smoke from the fire in the hearth would blow back into the room. From the bedroom windows she could see the raging heaving sea with white crests on the waves and the dark ominous clouds as far as the horizon. Being married to Bert for a great number of years, she had grown use to him going out in all weather, but today it seemed different, it wasn't just a high wind, it was violent. She glanced at the tall grandfather clock standing in the corner of the room. Eleven o'clock. He'd told her he would be back by ten o'clock. She made a cup of coffee and settled down with a magazine and awaited his arrival.

By mid-day the ferocity of the wind outside had quietened considerably, although clouds still raced across the sky, but Bert had not made his appearance. Uneasiness and anxiety began to creep into her mind. Bert never missed his meals. By two o'clock there was only one thing to do – go to the harbour and see for herself what had caused the delay.

Butch the black Labrador dog was curled in his basket but began to stir as Mary reached for her coat and scarf hanging from a peg behind the door. Once outside she realised how violent the wind had been. The road was littered with papers, wooden boxes, tree branches, roof tiles and wooden fencing scattered about. Television aerials and telephone wires were hanging down at alarming angles. Windows in holiday cottages were blown in, chimney pots lay smashed in the road. The whole scene looked like a battlefield.

Mary Watts was a tall slim grey-haired woman well into her sixties leading a healthy active life. Her day consisted of looking after the cottage, preparing meals, and in her spare time devoting her time to painting watercolours of scenes around the island. Several of her paintings had been converted into view cards and sold in the local shops.

Butch was unaware of the situation as he pranced about in the long wet grass in front of her. Nearing the harbour she began to search the horizon for any sign of the *Northern Pride*, expecting to see Bert going about his business as usual.

A handful of people were already on the harbour looking at the damage caused by the vicious storm. In one of the moored boats she heard hammering. Only three boats were alongside the quay. In the thick black mud left behind by the receding tide, wooden boxes, crab pots and pieces of canvas sail lay strewn about. One boat had a large hole in its side ripped open by the force of the wind. Another green-painted boat lay on its side, smashed in the mud. Windows in some boats were broken and sails hung helplessly flapping in the gentle breeze. It was not a picture Mary wanted to see, her heart sank.

As if possessed with a sixth sense, Butch kept close to Mary's side as she walked towards the sound of hammering.

'Hello!' she shouted over the side of the quay to the boat where the work was being carried out.

'Hello there . . .' she repeated.

The hammering stopped. A full-bearded man appeared through the doorway of the boat's cabin.

'I'm looking for Bert Watts,' she said, moving closer to the edge of the quay. 'Have you seen him?'

'Bert Watts – the *Northern Pride*?'

'Yes, he went out early this morning.'

'Good God – You mean he went out in that storm?'

'Yes, he should have been back hours ago.'

'Maybe if he saw it coming he pulled in somewhere . . . but I'm surprised he went out in that lot.'

5

Mary walked slowly back home, unclear in her mind what to do next, turning round from time to time expecting to see Bert calling her. Her mind in turmoil, she found a slither of hope in the fact that he might have pulled in somewhere, perhaps damaged and needing repairs, but safe.

Arriving back at the cottage, the warmth from the fire greeted her, wrapping itself around her as she discarded her scarf and coat. Butch curled up in his basket unaware of the crisis about to hit his home.

Mary glanced at the grandfather clock. It showed 3.45 pm. Bert was now nearly six hours overdue for his meal. She paced the room, clearly agitated. 'I must phone Robert,' she thought. Moving over to the small table on which stood the telephone, she dialled his number – silence. The horror of being cut off from the outside world sent a feeling of panic through her. The telephone lines were down and there was no way she could contact him. She was in this alone. In another few hours the tide would be in and the whole island would be isolated with no communication with the outside world.

There had been more rain during the afternoon, the clouds building up as the evening drew near, the wind just a whisper. It was as if the great beast of the morning was now exhausted. In the evening Mary walked down to the harbour again. A half moon broke through the clouds and shone down onto the road of blue steel and danced on the water in the harbour. She stood looking out to sea hoping for a mast light to appear at the harbour entrance, clinging to the hope that Bert had sought shelter. But somewhere in her heart she knew he was not coming back.

Still reluctant to leave she paced along the quay, scanning the night, listening to the many sounds as she got steadily colder. Somewhere in the far distance a dog was barking. On the mound where the castle stood sheep were bleating, a bird call rang out, stars appeared through the gaps in the clouds. She turned and saw the lights in the cottages she had left behind, whose occupants' lives had not been changed by the storm. She suddenly felt very alone.

TWO

Dr Robert Watts returned home for the evening and was greeted by his wife's opening remarks about the violent storm in the early hours of the day which had swept across southern England, spilling out into the North Sea.

'I have tried to ring your mother but there is no reply, the phone is dead.'

'See what is on the evening news on TV,' he replied.

Robert Watts was the only son of Bert and Mary Watts. He was tall and good looking, married to Gemma whom he had known since schooldays. They had two children, Graham and Zoe. Their home was set in beautiful surroundings in the Charnwood Forest area in Leicestershire.

As a boy Robert Watts was a loner, he spent all his spare time on the beach on Lindisfarne picking up stones, shells and other objects catching his eye that might be worth identification on his return home. When he was transferred to the senior school on the mainland he lived with his recently widowed aunt, returning home to the island at the end of each term. He surprised everyone when he gained entrance into Edinburgh University, leaving with a PhD in geology and archeology.

Mary was proud of her son Robert becoming a doctor, a far cry from fishing or farming on the island where he once lived. His wife Gemma was also at senior school on the mainland, along with Jackie Reynolds the head girl, now married to a junior director of an electronics firm in Berwick-on Tweed. It was through Jackie that Gemma and Robert met many years ago. All three were now in their thirties. Dr Watts was previously engaged to be married to Linda Schofield, a geography lecturer, when he was working and living in London. Three months before the intended wedding Linda had arranged to take twelve students to China for studies of Eastern culture. 'There are thirteen in the party with me,' she said to Robert before she left, 'I hope that is not an omen!' and she laughed. On 28 July 1976 China had one of the biggest earthquakes in its history. It caused a fracture 150 kilometres long in the early hours, killing 250.000 people between Peking and Tangshan, a large industrial area. Linda was in that area at the time. He never saw her again. The Chinese Government were slow to release information of news or details, as its communist leaders were particularly anxious to minimise the impact in view of the political turmoil at that time.

At a garden party given by Jackie Reynolds at her home in Berwick-on-Tweed in 1980, she had invited as many old school pals to the party as she could contact. Gemma Barclay and Dr Robert Watts were amongst the guests.

Some eighteen months later, Robert and Gemma were married at Chorley church in Lancashire, the home town of Gemma's parents.

After a short period of living in a London flat, they moved into the Midlands to a newly converted barn about a mile from Rothley in the Charnwood Forest area.

'I'll ring the police and explain our situation,' said Robert, reassuring her all might be all right.

Gemma returned to the kitchen and continued with the evening meal. She could hear Robert speaking on the phone in the hall. Eventually he returned, looking very solemn. 'Not a lot of use I'm afraid,' he said. 'All they could tell me was some property has been damaged together with damage to several boats in the harbour, and that one man is still missing.'

'Oh Robert, You don't think . . .'

'I don't know Gemma, maybe I should go up there and see for myself.'

After his evening meal Robert set off to drive through the night to Lindisfarne to clear his mind of all notions and fears. The half moon shone in a clear sky making the driving a little easier, but it was not a journey he would have chosen. Along the A1 north his Volvo car ate up the miles. There was no evidence of any damage en-route as far as he could see, so any damage had to be nearer the east coast. Thoughts passed through his mind as he travelled on, remembering on one occasion telling his father he needed a new engine instead of using every spare moment taking parts off and cleaning them, then replacing them.

'Costs money, lad,' he would say, 'can't afford it – not just yet, but one day we'll see.'

His father was a stubborn, strong-willed tough kind of man, gentle in many ways, but strong, generous and kind. The kind of person you could rely on for help if needed.

When Robert was at home Bert had found immense pleasure in his finds from the beach. Having spent many years **on** the sea, he had never really realised the interest and treasures that it unfolded on the beach.

'Don't become a fisherman,' was his advice to his son. 'Get yourself a proper job.'

The car sped on mile after mile, occasionally Robert would inwardly curse the dazzling lights of oncoming traffic. The more he though of the safety of his father, the more he remembered some of his sayings: 'You don't fool with sea.' Being torpedoed twice during the war taught him that much. 'The sea is far too strong to mess with,' and 'Treat it with the utmost respect.' With those sayings still echoing in his mind, Robert was pretty sure his father would not be on the sea in that storm.

Another hour on and Robert was beginning to feel the strain. And then in the distance a faint streak of light appeared on the horizon in the east, dawn was breaking on another day. He glanced at the clock on the dash, and saw that it showed just after six o'clock. It would be another hour at least before the sun rose, by which time he could be on the causeway going over to the island, if all went well.

Turning off the main A1 road, the large orange sun faced him as he drove towards the causeway connecting the mainland to the island. He had got the tide wrong. The water was still very high. How could he be so stupid. He glanced at his wristwatch – it was just after 7.15 am. Blast! It would be at least another four hours before there was any chance of crossing. Why had it not occurred to him to check the time of the tide before he set out? In the past whenever he had taken his family to visit his parents, he always made sure he got the crossing time correct.

He put it down to confusion and anxiety and was now paying the price. At least four hours to wait. What does one do for four hours sitting in a car waiting for the tide to recede? Jackie Reynolds – Jackie lived at Berwick only nine miles away, maybe he could call on her until it was time to cross.

Travelling along the road towards Berwick-on-Tweed Robert could see broken garden fences, television aerials hanging down, tree branches strewn about, all evidence of a great storm. Driving into the town of

Berwick whole shop windows were blown in, roof slates lay smashed in the road leaving gaping holes in the house roofs, papers and litter piled up in corners. It must have been some storm, he thought.

He drew up outside Jackie's house, a tall three storey modern town house, and mounted the two steps up to the front door and rang the bell. Adjusting his tie as he waited, eventually he heard footsteps approaching in the hallway. The look of utter surprise as Jackie opened the door and saw Robert standing before her compensated for all the long hours of driving and the disappointment in getting the tide wrong. She looked stunning as ever. 'Robert! What a lovely surprise, is Gemma with you?' She looked about her.

'No Jackie, Gemma is not with me.' He kissed her on the cheek.

'Come in and tell my why you have come,' she said opening the door wider. He followed her along the hallway into a room at the rear of the house.

'You must excuse the untidiness, I have only just finished the ironing.' She beckoned him towards a chair. 'Sit down and tell me.'

Robert related his story in full as she listened intently, latching onto every word he spoke.

'So until you get over there, you don't know what has happened, but I can tell you it was a very bad storm, I thought my windows were coming in. It was still blowing hard when Roslin went out to catch the school bus.'

'Where is John then?' he asked.

Jackie shifted and looked uneasy for a moment, then casting eyes downwards she began to tell her story.

'John and I are not at our best at the moment, Robert. His firm has opened a new branch in Switzerland, in Bern. He was made a full director of the firm and put in charge of setting up and running the new branch over there. We were both thrilled, obviously, but when he told me he was going on his own and leaving Roslin and me behind, you can imagine my feelings. He pays all the bills – granted, but what kind of married life is that for me?'

The room fell silent. Robert eventually broke it. 'How long has he been gone?' he asked.

'Eight months now, and in all that time he has phoned me once and written to me once.'

Robert remained speechless. He had not come to hear Jackie's troubles although he sympathised with her. He thought she was far too attractive to leave behind. Tall, blonde, elegant and always well dressed, a tidy neat figure – he admired her, perhaps too much.

'Forgive me Robert I'm so sorry to inflict my problems on you at this time when you are worrying what has happened to your parents, would you like a coffee?'

'Yes please, Jackie.'

She moved and crossed the room towards the kitchen, but not before brushing her hand on his as he sat in the chair.

There was a noise as something dropped in the hall.

'That will be the morning paper Robert. I'll bring it in.'

'Oh my God,' she exclaimed as she re-entered the room reading the paper. 'Yesterday's storm was a hurricane!'

Robert's heart missed a beat. 'A hurricane?' he repeated.

'Here read it for yourself.'

The headlines read: **HURRICANE HITS BRITAIN**.

Robert's hand shook as he read the account of havoc caused, with extensive damage to property and the countryside as it travelled across the southern part of Britain. Firemen had lost their lives when a tree crushed their vehicle. Six of the seven oak trees in the town of that name were destroyed. Channel crossings were cancelled, all flights from Heathrow, Gatwick and Stansted were stopped. The cost of the damage could run into millions.

'Good God,' he said looking up from the newspaper, 'it was a pretty serious storm by all accounts, Jackie.'

'I knew there was a very high wind blowing but I didn't know it was a hurricane.'

'I'm more unsettled now, I can't wait to get over there – blasted tide . . .'

He left his chair and walked over to the window. Jackie followed him and stood behind him holding him round the waist. 'I'll get my tide book and see when it is fit for you to cross.'

'Thanks Jackie.'

She left the room. He started to pace up and down, his thoughts in turmoil. Surely his father would not go out in a hurricane? He questioned himself. Was he over re-acting? When he did finally arrive over the other side, would he find his father sitting in his favourite chair with Mary working in the kitchen and Butch asleep in his basket? – If only he could get over there. Jackie re-entered the room holding a small book of tide times. 'Here you are Robert.' Opening it she said, 'October – there see for yourself.'

She handed him the book and stood very close beside him.

He glanced at his wristwatch. 'Just my luck, another four and a half hours before I can even start to think of crossing.'

'I'm so sorry Robert, you must feel terrible.'

'I cannot even phone, the workmen will not be able to get there to do repairs. What a situation Jackie. I feel helpless.'

'You had better sit down and I'll get you something to eat, you must be hungry, and then later I will take you to a little bistro I know before you go off.'

'Don't do anything elaborate for me I'm not all that hungry, I'm too worried.'

'You've still got to eat – otherwise your mother will be worrying about you.' She laughed and left the room. Robert picked up the paper again and sat on the settee to read, with the smell of her perfume in his nostrils.

THREE

Robert drove his car across the still wet causeway trying to minimise the amount of water he was picking up. The morning sun glistening on the wet mud left behind by the tide was a familiar sight to him. Guillemots, Gannets, Plovers, Oyster Catchers and Gulls wheeling and screaming as they busied themselves picking up food from the black mud brought back memories of happier days. Eventually the car mounted the road into the village leaving the noise of birds behind. Lindisfarne lay wounded. About him were wrecked garden fencing, chimney pots, glass from windows blown out by the force of the high wind, television aerials hung twisted and limp from their moorings. Gaping holes appeared in the roofs of several cottages, papers and pieces of wood, oil barrels and tin cans rolled about. Robert stood outside his car looking about him before opening the small once white painted wooden gate leading to the side door of the cottage 'Sea Winds'. The small front garden was a mixture of cultivated and wild flowers interlaced with thorny bracken and white convolvulus. The cottage seemed strangely quiet as he opened the door slowly after first knocking, knowing his mother rarely kept the door locked during daylight hours. Butch was the first to greet him, stirring from his basket.

'Robert!' cried Mary, half turning in his direction as Butch gave a quiet bark. ''Thank God you have come.'

Mary hugged her son tightly. He could feel her sobbing as she gently shook, holding on to him. Breaking away from him she told him of the events of the previous day. First how his father had listened to the weather forecast before setting off, telling her would be back for his mid-day meal as usual. She sobbed then continued, telling him how she went down to the harbour and saw all the wreckage and destruction, and how someone working on a boat was surprised that anyone would go out in that kind of weather.

'I went down again in the evening, just hoping I could see his mast light coming in, thinking he might have put in somewhere. The phone line is dead, I couldn't get in touch with anyone, not even you Robert.'

She sat down on the chair facing the fireplace, Butch got out of his basket and sat looking up at her. 'I did manage to see Mr Thomas this morning, he lives round the back there, he was off to Berwick market, said he would inform the police and ask them to tell the coastguard. It is very awkward not having the phone at a time like this.'

The sound of heavy lorries going past made Robert look out of the window.

'It looks as if the telephone people are here mum – Oh, and the police. Something is being done at last. I first heard about it on the TV news last night, I tried to ring you to see what the situation was, when we saw the damage done I said to Gemma I must go up there and see what is what, but I got the tide wrong like a fool, so I drove over to Jackie Reynolds' in Berwick. She gave me something to eat until it was time to cross over.'

He moved over to Butch and stroked him.

'I'll go down to the harbour myself. You can come too old chap.'

Dr Robert Watts had been on the island two hours walking briskly in the fresh morning air towards the harbour with Butch leading the way. Picking his way through the pools of rain water left behind by the storm, he could see a number of people standing around in groups, some uniformed others in casual attire. Police cars, vans, private cars and the coastguard's vehicle lined the entrance. His father's old pick-up truck stood a few feet away from them. A white and blue plastic streamer was stretched across the road with a uniformed police officer standing close by, obviously an attempt to keep the public out.

As he approached, the police officer left his post and walked towards him, and held up his hand. 'Hold it right there,' he commanded.

Robert ignored his command and kept walking. The officer quickened his pace and was now only feet away. 'You cannot go to the harbour, sir.'

'I believe you are looking for my father, Bert Watts?' was Robert's reply, still walking.

'And you are?' asked the officer, now alongside him.

'Robert Watts, Dr Robert Watts, his son.'

'Oh I'm sorry.' With that he broke into a trot towards the group of police, two of whom approached and stood talking to him. As Robert got closer to them the more senior officer left the others and walked towards him. 'Good morning Doctor,' he started. 'I understand your father is the missing person?'

'Yes, that's right – Bert Watts.'

'Good God, I'm sorry. Tell me Doctor, was your father an experienced sailor?'

Robert stopped in his tracks and glared into the officer's eyes.

'EXPERIENCED!' came the retorted reply. 'Of course he was experienced, the sea was his life, he knew nothing else.'

'No, don't get me wrong, sir,' pleaded the officer, ' I asked because the weather yesterday was exceptional. We had a hurricane.'

'A hurricane, who mentioned a hurricane? I knew it was windy, granted, but he would never set out to sea in hurricane! If there had been the smallest chance of danger my father would not set out to sea – he had the greatest respect for it. He was torpedoed twice during the war. He knew what he was doing.' Robert began to walk away towards the harbour.

'Then why *did* he set out in a hurricane?' the officer called out to him.

Robert stopped walking and turned round to face him. 'Was a hurricane warning given out on the radio yesterday?'

'I don't know.'

'Then find out, that is what you should be doing now, not just standing around. Who failed to give out a warning, putting people's lives at risk? What was the met office doing? Standing about is not doing anything!'

He stormed off, leaving the officer standing there. As he approached the main group, he was greeted with ' 'morning' and a nod of the head as he passed by them onto the quay.

Looking about him he could see the damage inflicted on the boats. One boat lay half submerged in the thick black mud on its side, others had broken masts, torn sails, port windows blown out, equipment strewn about in the harbour mud. Hammering could be heard coming from a boat further along. A group of four or five men turned and looked in his direction as he approached.

A voice from the group called out, 'Is that Robert?' It belonged to Alf Everitt. Holding out his hand in greeting, he left the group and stepped forward.

'Hello Alf,' answered Robert. 'Good to see you again.'

'Aye. Pity about your dad. I saw him off yesterday morning.'

'Did you? What kind of mood was he in Alf? Did he make any comment about the weather?'

'Yeah, said it wa' a bit breezy.'

'Is that all?'

'More or less. I said why don't you wait a bit, go out later. He said summat like he'd got to make a living and he'd been out in worse.' Alf stood shaking his head in disbelief. 'He said it would blow the cobwebs away, or summat like that.'

'No mention of a hurricane then?'

'No just breezy. Bert wouldn't go out in a hurricane man, he weren't daft. He wa' fishing an' I wa' farming before me and I've been retired a long time now.'

'Try telling that to that officer up there Alf. Who are all those people standing about?'

'That'll be the press and men from council as well as police.'

'What good are they doing there? Like a bunch of vultures waiting.'

An army lorry carrying about a dozen soldiers drew up. After a brief consultation with the police officer, the soldiers split up and set off different directions.

Alf returned to his group of friends.

'Sorry to hear about your dad,' said one of the group. 'He's probably OK. He's been having trouble with his engine lately so perhaps he pulled in somewhere, but wi' phone lines down we don't know.'

Robert half smiled at that last remark.

'He wa' a tough old bugger, I remember once me and Jack Mason were looking down at Bert on his boat from the quayside and talking to him as he were coiling some ropes, suddenly he lost his balance and went arse over 'ead in water, we both laughed like hell and had to pull 'im out, should 'ave 'eard 'is language.'

'I'll bet,' said Robert.

It was about mid-day when he arrived back at the cottage as a helicopter flew low over the roof tops before turning and going out to sea.

Mary was in the kitchen peeling potatoes ready for lunch when Robert walked in.

'Plenty of activity now down there, police, press, army, they all see it as a spectacle – news to sell their papers. I expect that is how it will be for the next few days.'

He turned and looked at his mother, tears ran down her cheeks.

'Sorry mum, I didn't mean to say days.' He cursed himself for that last remark. 'Is there a spare set of car keys for the truck?'

'Yes in the drawer in the corner cabinet.' She wiped her eyes on her apron. 'Are you going to bring it back, then?'

'Yes might as well, no point in leaving it there. Is the phone on yet? Men are working up the poles with cables out there.'

He walked over and picked up the phone, but got a buzzing sound. 'No it's not on yet.'

'Maybe it will be on tonight, then you can ring Gemma.' Mary said from the kitchen.

'Yes, sure.'

The pick-up truck stood where Bert had left it on that early breezy morning, now covered with leaves and debris from the storm. He could see soldiers climbing amongst the rocks along the beach looking for any sign or clue of evidence that might shed light on the disappearance of a man lost at sea. Butch jumped into the truck's cab as soon as Robert opened the door, a practice he had done over the years. Inserting the key in the ignition the truck sprang into life, drawing attention to him, as reporters and police turned and looked in his direction. One policeman was about to approach him but was called back by a more senior officer.

As he turned the truck round and was about to leave the harbour, a newspaperman approached him.

I understand it is your father that is missing?' he said holding onto the handle of the truck's door. 'I'm very sorry'.

'Are you?' Robert replied. 'I know you have a job to do, but somebody, somewhere, didn't do theirs.'

'What do you mean?' asked the reporter.

'The weather office. They failed to see a hurricane coming, how's that for modern technology?' Robert leaned out of the truck window and pointed upwards towards the sky. 'We can see a man walking on the moon but we can't see a bloody hurricane under our nose. How is that for progress?'

Robert drove off leaving the reporter standing in the road.

Arriving back at the cottage he parked the truck alongside the cottage off the road and stood looking at the overgrown state of the garden, then entered.

'Can you see to the fire while I put this washing out please,' said Mary from the kitchen.

'Sure!'

The weather that morning was calm, the sun was trying to break through the cumulus clouds in a kind of hide and seek. The gentle wind caused no more than a ripple on the sea, in sharp contrast to the previous day. It seemed the elements had overworked themselves and now lay exhausted, and this was their rest period.

17

Robert attended to the fire then stood looking out of the window. Everywhere was strangely quiet and still, not even the shrill call of gulls or the movement of vans and lorries broke the stillness. His thoughts went back to the last time he was in this cottage – last summer. Gemma and the children were with him. It was a happy carefree time. He turned away from the window and sat in an easy chair, closed his eyes and sank into oblivion.

He was awakened by a knock on the door and Butch barking.

'All right mum, I'll get it,' he called to Mary in the kitchen.

Alf Everitt stood at the door. 'Hello, is Mary in?'

'Yes Alf, come in,' Robert said opening the door wider for him to enter. 'Mum, it's Alf for you.'

Mary entered the room drying her hands on a towel, 'Hello Alf,' she greeted.

'I had to come and see you Mary, I wa' the last to see 'im,' he said awkwardly. 'I just can't believe it, I'm very sorry.'

'Thank you Alf, nobody knows what's happened yet, come in and have a cup of tea.'

Alf entered the room, Butch following him in, wagging his tail.

'So you were the last person to see him then?' Mary said going back into the kitchen to put the kettle on.

'Yes Mary, I was out early – as you know I can't settle since Sally went. It were a fresh mornin', a bit blowy, but it didn't seem to worry 'im.' He sat stroking Butch who lay at his feet. 'He said "Bit fresh today," I said, "Yeah, why don't you wait a bit, go out later?" "Nah," he said, "got to make a living, I've been out in worse." I helped him cast off, he just waved and that were the last I saw of 'im.' He shook his head. 'I can't believe it.'

'Bert sat having his breakfast as usual,' said Mary, 'he sat listening to the weather forecast on the radio then looked at the clock, "I'd better get off, tide's up now."' She stood in the kitchen doorway waiting for the kettle to boil.

'We are just hoping he saw a change in the weather and put in somewhere Alf, but with the phones being off we don't know, all we can do is wait.'

'He wa' far too experienced to do ought daft,' Alf said. 'I do know he'd been having a bit of trouble wi' engine, but he could 'andle it.'

The noise of a helicopter flying low overhead stopped the conversation.

* * *

Four days had passed since the storm, with no further news of Bert Watts. The police tape had been removed from the harbour entrance, allowing the workers and members of the public access once more. Robert had phoned Gemma every night, keeping her updated now the phones had been restored. He had suggested that Mary go back with him, but this was flatly refused. She wanted to stay there – just in case!

It was an overcast day, huge banks of nimbus cloud overlapping cumulus had eliminated any chance of the sun getting through or blue sky being seen. A breeze had sprung up from the east. It was a little after ten o'clock in the morning. Robert was putting on his anorak ready to take Butch for his usual walk. As he opened the door he was confronted by a police officer about to knock on the door.

'Good morning,' said the officer.

Robert noticed how young he appeared to be, glancing towards the gate he could see a policewoman sitting in the car with a bunch of papers in her hand. The officer moved uneasily. 'We believe some wreckage has been found, would you come along with us for identification?'

'Where?' asked Robert, his pulse racing.

'Further along the coast, other side of Chiswick towards Borewell. A fishing boat saw it and brought it ashore. The tide is down obviously, so we can make it there and back before high tide again.'

''Yes. Thanks.' Turning towards his mother who had heard the officer's remarks, he said, 'We'll be as quick as possible.'

Robert sat looking out of the police car window as it crossed the causeway. The vast expanse of mud left behind by the tide was a haven for food of all varieties of waders and sea birds. He sat directly behind the policewoman in the back of the car and noticed her long blonde hair plaited down her back, reminding him of Gemma's. He guessed she was about thirty-three years old; far too attractive to be a policewoman he thought, a model would be more apt. She turned round to speak to him. Her complexion was flawless, her teeth white and perfect, and with her blue eyes she was perfect. He envied the officer for having such an attractive working companion all day in the line of duty. The answers to her questions were noted and put down on the clipboard she had resting on her knees.

Turning off the A1 after thirty minutes or so, the car passed over a cobbled area and came to a halt in a yard stacked high with crab pots and wooden boxes, rusting buoys, anchor chains and discarded engines and broken ship's rudders. A long red-bricked building with a rusty tin roof was the main work shed, its doors stood wide open. Further along the yard another red brick building with huge wooden doors stood heavily padlocked.

The officer was the first out of the car. Straightening his jacket he set out towards the opened doors. Robert was the last out of the car and followed the policewoman across the yard, noticing how slim and upright she was with an elegant walk.

A short bearded man appeared at the doorway rubbing his hands on an oily cloth. He wore a once blue pullover, now covered with grease and oil stains. The officer talked to him in lowered inaudible tones. Eventually he turned and walked back to Robert and his assistant. The old man walked further up the yard to the second brick building and began unlocking the large padlocks securing a huge heavy wooden door which creaked as it was opened.

The policewoman, a clip board in one hand, offered Robert support by taking his arm with a smile and leading him towards the wide opened door with the old man standing beside it.

The door creaked slightly in the wind as the three entered the cold, almost dark interior. The old man searched along the interior wall until he found the light switch.

Two unshaded lights appeared hanging down from the wooden beams across the room.

'Are you all right?' asked the policewoman.

'I don't know,' replied Robert. 'It feels kind of strange.'

'I know,' she replied, 'it is never a pleasant experience to ask anyone to identify artifacts once owned by someone you loved.'

The interior felt cold, damp and draughty. The roof was of corrugated iron with gaping holes allowing the wind and rain to enter, leaving pools of rainwater on the grease trodden floor; along one side of the building was a long wooden bench on which stood a vice and bench drill, tins of grease and paint and a grindstone. An out of date calendar displaying scantily dressed girls in erotic poses hung on the wall. Cobwebs stretched across the bench and on the filthy unwashed windows. Engine parts lay scattered about the interior. In one corner stood an air compressor with a spray gun attached. Ships' parts were everywhere, rudders and masts stood propped against the wall and the rank smell of oil and paraffin made Robert feel sick. A long wooden ladder hung along the wall and coiled hemp ropes were everywhere together with fishing nets and buoys.

He could almost feel the policewoman shudder as she stood looking elegant amongst this untidy, filthy smelly interior. And then, as if hit a violent blow with a sledge-hammer, he saw beyond any doubt a large section of a once painted white boat leaning against the wall with the name *Northern Pride* painted on it.

Robert reeled, the voice of the officer grew fainter, the interior began to sway and undulate. He felt sick, sweat broke out on his forehead. The policewoman saw him reeling and immediately held on to him. 'Hold on Doctor,' she said. 'Sit on this box.' She brought the wooden box forward giving him assistance. He looked ghastly, his breathing was heavy and with a shaking finger he pointed to the boat section leaning against the wall.

'You identify that part of the boat?' asked the officer.

'Yes I do,' was the answer. 'That was his boat.' He sat with his head in his hands. He knew the purpose of his visit, but still the reality of the facts facing him left him quite unprepared – it was a tremendous shock.

The policewoman was entering notes on her clipboard and talking to the old man just feet away. 'The chap wants to know what you want doing with it?' she said walking over to where he sat on the box and putting her hand on his shoulder. He looked up at her. She smiled.

'Tell him I want it,' he whispered.

'You are sure?'

'Yes. Tell him I will call for it tomorrow, I'll pay him something for it. Where did he find it?'

'About a quarter of a mile off shore yesterday evening.'

Driving back to Lindisfarne Robert's mind was full of unanswered questions.

1. If his father had put out to sea on what he said to Alf Everitt, 'It's a bit breezy,' nothing unfamiliar with that, but surely he would have seen the build up of clouds and made for base. Did he see the signs and head for home? Was he on the way back home, did his engine fail? Since no-one was with him, we will never know the answer to that question.

2. The boat was smashed to pieces. Did it break up with the force of the waves before his father lost his life, or was his father already drowned in the sea and the boat break up afterwards? He would never know the answer to that either.

3. Would the sea ever give his body up somewhere? Fishing boats and trawlers when landing their nets and discovering a body amongst the catch are presented with a big problem. The disastrous effect on their

sales together with time lost attending an inquest can leave them with little choice – put it back and say nothing.

Would he ever know the answers? How would his mother cope on her own?

Occasionally the policewoman would turn round to him with a smile. 'Are you all right?'

'Yes thanks,' was the reply, looking out of the window at the weak sun shining on the wet mud in the estuary and the scores of birds circling and landing in search of food, something he had witnessed a thousand times leaving him exhilarated at the sight, but today it held little interest, his thoughts were elsewhere.

He now had to break the news to his mother.

Arriving back at the cottage as he got out of the car the policewoman came to stand beside him. She held his arm and smiled. 'Perhaps we will meet again, take care.'

He thanked them both for taking him over to identify his father's boat, and stood and watched as the car disappeared from sight.

Mary sat motionless throughout Robert's report, her eyes looked straight through him. When he had finished she leaned back in her chair and stared at the ceiling for a full two minutes, then cried out, 'Where is he?' and buried her head in her hands and sobbed.

'I don't know mum, I don't know, but I'm fetching that part of the boat tomorrow, I'm bringing it back where it belongs, I don't want it kicking about in a dirty scrap yard like a piece of junk . . .'

The next morning was wet. It had drizzled all night, the sky was a uniform grey with no hint of a break. Robert was backing the truck out of the driveway as Alf was passing.

''Morning Robert, any news?' he asked.

Robert brought him up to date and told him he was going over to pick the wreckage up.

'See ya,' called Alf as Robert pulled away.

Driving across the causeway on this wet morning did nothing to improve his mind. Dark rugged nimbus clouds moved about the sky whipping up a strong north east wind as the truck lurched from side to side splashing through the pools of water left behind by the tide. Once on the main road he made good time, in under an hour he was approaching the boatyard, driving over the cobbled area. Bringing the truck to a halt as near to the outbuilding as possible, he was met by the same old bearded man in the same old oily blue jumper. He recognised Robert immediately and turned to unlock the big wooden door.

'It's pretty heavy,' he said, 'it'll take two.'

Between them they managed to get the boat section onto the truck.

'Bad business this,' said the old man. 'I think I met your father once a long time ago. Came to me for some part for 'is boat, I've just recognised his truck.'

Robert pulled out his wallet. 'Will twenty pounds be all right?'

'Aye, I thank ya,' he said, touching his forehead as a salute. 'Kind o'ya. I'll see ya out.'

He moved to the gate entrance and signalled Robert safely through.

Robert drove the truck back to the island and parked it at the side of the cottage. Mary looked searchingly at him as he entered.

'Well, have you brought it back?' she asked, sitting down to hear all about it.

'Yes Mum, it is on the truck, but I need someone to help me off with it.'

'Where are you going to put it?'

'Frankly mum, I don't know, but I did not want it kicking about in an old boatyard. At least it is something of his.' He moved over to the window and stood looking out. 'It belongs here.'

'Oh Robert, why did it have to happen?'

'That is a question I keep asking myself. He knew the sea, it was his life, he respected it, he wouldn't fool with it. So what went wrong?'

Mary shook her head.

'Did he see the storms clouds gathering? Did that blasted engine let him down? Did he miss the vital weather report and went out too early?'

Three days had passed since the wreckage had been retrieved and placed amongst the crab pots at the bottom of the garden as a memorial. There had been no further news of more wreckage being found or any sighting of a body. The police and newspapermen had left the scene and to some extent the village had returned to normality again.

Meanwhile Jackie had telephoned Gemma in Leicestershire, having read about it in the local newspaper, giving her the account of the search for a body. Knowing that Robert was still on the island she had decided to give him a visit.

23

Mary was putting on a brave face. 'There is nothing anyone can do now only wait and see if he turns up.' She walked into the kitchen. 'You might as well go back. You have a family to look after. I'll be all right on my own.'

Jackie Reynolds' car drew up outside about noon, and she threw her arms around Robert's neck as soon as she entered the door. Once inside she explained how she had heard on the radio that a local fisherman was still missing after the storm. When she realised who that person in question was, she had telephoned Gemma, who filled her in and told her that Robert was still on the island.

'Pleased you've come.' said Robert. 'It is a very difficult time for both of us right now. Part of the boat was washed up and I went over yesterday to collect it and get it back here where it belongs.'

'What can I say to both of you except that I am truly, truly very sorry. I remember him at your wedding Robert, many years ago now.'

'Sit down Jackie,' said Mary. 'You want a coffee?'

'That would be nice, thank you.'

Robert looked hard at Jackie and wondered how a man could leave such an good-looking wife behind and not see her for months. She was very attractive, the way she moved, always well dressed and immaculate, stunningly elegant with her dark eyes and brown hair, well proportioned features together with her intelligence and beautiful speaking voice and natural charm which made her stand out in a crowd. Robert was finding it difficult to keep his gaze away from her. He was overwhelmed by the sight of her well shaped legs, her neat hairstyle, lovely complexion and her well developed figure.

It was Jackie who broke the silence. 'When are you going back home?' she asked.

'I have to stay on until we hear something which we both dread, that is if it ever happens, then there will be an inquest and finally a funeral.'

'So it could be weeks?'

'I've no idea, we are in limbo now, I'll give it another couple of weeks or so then if nothing happens I shall go back.'

'Then perhaps you would both like to come over to me and have a meal?'

'That is very kind of you, I would like that, but whether mum will come is another matter.'

Mary returned with the coffee on a tray and placed it on the table. Butch stirred from his basket and began to stretch himself.

'All right, Butch,' said Mary, 'he'll take you soon.'

'Jackie,' Robert began, 'you have about four hours before the tide is up again – perhaps you would like a walk to the harbour with Butch, I have to take him out.'

'Mmm, that would be nice.'

'You two go on your own, I'll stop here. Robert needs a break with some younger company.'

Robert felt proud walking with Jackie by his side. Butch was quite happy just being out and foraging in the long grass in front of them. All around them was the sweet smell of freshness after the past few days of incessant rain. They passed several birdwatchers with telescopes and cameras. Men dressed in oilskins loading boxes onto trucks turned their heads as they walked past, some giving a wolf whistle as they eyed Jackie up and down.

From inside one of the boats moored alongside the quay the noise of hammering was heard, and then a voice rang out,

'I don't believe it. Dr Watts I presume!' The voice belonged to a tall, weather-beaten face which appeared from the cabin of a boat leaning hard against the quay wall.

Both turned in the direction of the voice to see a happy grinning face under a blue knitted woollen hat.

'Good Lord,' said Robert, 'I never thought I would see you here, I thought you were in Africa?'

'Not any more dear chap, not any more.' The tall figure of Jack Mason clambered up the iron ladder attached to the quay wall holding out his hand in greeting.

'Jack Mason – meet my friend of many years and friend of the family.'

'Sorry to hear about your dad, Robert. Rotten luck. Whyever did he go out on a day like that?'

'Good question Jack, that's what I want to know.'

'There was nothing on the radio that morning about a hurricane, I listen every morning.'

'Thank you Jack, that is what I have been wanting to hear – so why was there no warning?'

'I thought it strange, Robert, when I heard what happened, poor Bert. I should have gone out myself that morning but I had a touch of diarrhoea.'

'I wish he had, I'll never know why he went out that day.'

'He will be sadly missed,' Jack said, looking at the ground. 'Not just as a fisherman, a mate or anything like that but as a man sincere in everything he did – a man of principles and a man you could trust.'

'Thank you for that, Jack.' Robert squeezed his arm.

On the way back from the quay Robert told Jackie how Jack Mason once lived in Africa and worked for MacFisheries, stationed at Entebbe on the banks of Lake Victoria. Jack always claimed that he and two others were responsible for positioning the home-made torpedo and raft which finally destroyed the German patrol boat on Lake Victoria in the film *The African Queen*, with Humphrey Bogart and Katharine Hepburn.

Jackie clung to Robert's arm on the way back, at times putting her head on his shoulder as they walked slowly with Butch leading the way. A pale sun began to make an appearance through a bank of clouds. Seagulls circled screaming overhead as Robert told her how he used to spend hours combing the shore for shells, stones or anything which he found interesting, then after identification arrange them on his shelves in his bedroom.

'Are they still there?' She asked.

'Most of them are.'

'I'd like to see them sometime.'

On the way back to the cottage Robert suggested a drink at the local, to which Jackie readily agreed. The interior of the pub was very basic, but cosy. A log fire burned in the big fireplace, brass plates hung from the walls, willow patterned plates adorned the walls on shelves. Oak beams stretched across the room, a dartboard hung on the end wall, on which four men were playing. A silence met them as they entered, all eyes turned towards them. Robert had a feeling of admiration as the men eyed Jackie up before resuming their play with raised eyebrows. In this one big room, ten people were enjoying a morning drink. Robert had met the present landlord on a previous occasion when on holiday with Gemma and the children. A small stout bespectacled man, he stepped forward offering Robert his hand in greeting. 'It's good to see you again,' he said as his wife came to join them.

'Meet a friend of my family,' said Robert, turning towards Jackie.

'How do you do,' said the wife of the landlord, and pulled Robert to one side. 'I was very sorry to hear about your father, it's terrible.'

'Thank you, we still don't know what happened.'

'What can I get you?' asked the landlord

Answering his request the landlord said, 'Sit down I'll bring them over to you.'

It was during this intimate period sitting at a corner table slowly sipping their drinks that Jackie dropped the bombshell. Her husband now living in Switzerland had been promoted to senior director and was in charge of setting up the company there. This next admission shook him. She told him he rarely came home not even on her or her daughter's birthday. He was sure that she would go into politics, having a good command of English, but she chose to become a secretary for a firm of solicitors in Berwick. Robert remained silent, listening to every word she spoke, inwardly he reflected on his association with this attractive, beautiful woman who was sitting next to him. He had known her since senior school days before going to university. She was head girl then, a no nonsense girl, strict but fair-minded.

At first both Jackie and her husband John had been very happy to celebrate her husband's success at being promoted to junior director. She had thrown a garden party at the house in Berwick. It was there Robert met his future wife Gemma Barclay. It was thought at the time that he had married too soon after Linda's death in the Chinese earthquake. But the marriage had worked out.

Robert sat listening to every word she spoke revealing some of the more intimate details of her married life which Robert found hard to believe. She was a beautiful woman, still dignified as she sat and opened her heart to him.

Robert put his hand on top of the table, which she readily accepted, and squeezed it gently as her eyes moistened. He sat looking at her shaking his head, finding it difficult to say anything. Suddenly a great cheer filled the room as a dart played scored a winning shot, bringing them both back to earth again.

'I don't know why I am telling you all this when you have your own troubles to contend with.'

'We all have our own cross to bear, Jackie, they say a trouble shared is a trouble . . .'

'I know, Robert.'

'I had no idea that things were that bad between you. If I can help in any way . . .'

'You can,' she interrupted. 'Just be there for me when I need support, someone to talk to, and promise me each time you come north you'll come and see me. You don't know what it means to me.'

'OK Jackie, I will.'

*   *   *

Entering the cottage to a warm fire was a welcome sight. Mary sat in her favourite chair reading her magazine with a cup of tea by her side.

'Enjoyed yourselves?' she asked.

'Yes thanks Mary, we called for a drink at the pub.'

'We saw Jack Mason at the harbour, he said he listened to the weather forecast that morning and no warning was given out about a hurricane,' Robert said, making sure Butch was settled in his basket.

'I don't understand,' said Mary, shaking her head.

'It is a great mystery and a great pity,' said Jackie. 'Anyway, thank you for having me but I must get back for Roslin's tea.' She shook Mary's hand and kissed her on the cheek. 'And YOU Robert, take care, I just hope things don't get any worse for you both, keep in touch – Bye.'

Robert followed her to her car outside. Before opening the door she turned and looked at him with a look of desire, then moved towards him and kissed him hard on the lips.

Robert stood motionless, watching her as the car engine sprang into life. With a smile and a wave of the hand she drove off.

Robert stood there watching the car drive away until it was just a speck in the distance.

FOUR

Driving back south down the A1 Robert's mind was in a state of confusion. He had already cancelled two lectures and his quarterly contribution for publication was under threat. Today he should have been in Prague. The thought of his mother being left alone so soon, and the events over the last two or three weeks, and his father still missing, did nothing to improve the situation. If his father's body did turn up there would be an inquest then a funeral to arrange. Life which can be a luxury, so lovely, is so easily broken, and when we turn and see the destruction, the agony, we ask ourselves questions: could this have been avoided? why must there be suffering? where did all the childhood laughter go? There are a few voices in the wilderness warning us of the dangers of life. We are repeatedly advised to avoid sexually transmitted diseases – but no one listens . . . not to destroy ourselves with drugs, nor to smoke, but people still carry on doing the same things. No one listened to the warning on the radio that morning when Bert Watts went missing because . . . none was given.

It was the second week in November. The clocks had already been put back an hour making the daylight shorter, not the type of weather to be travelling along the A1 for hours at a time with air frost and dazzling lights from oncoming traffic, after erratic sleep. It was beginning to have an effect on him.

The lights of 'Farcroft', the name of the converted barn building nestling in the quiet, peaceful countryside of Charnwood Forest in Leicestershire, were a welcome sight. With a sigh of relief he turned his car through the white painted field gate onto the gravelled path, pulling up outside the front door.

His wife Gemma was the first to throw her arms around him, kissing him repeatedly. 'It is good to have you back darling' she said. 'What a terrible time you have had.'

His two children joined in the welcome party with hugs and kisses,

29

Zoe telling him of her horseriding and Graham about his martial arts lessons, both at the same time.

'Quiet, children,' called Gemma, 'Daddy is tired, let him rest first and have a cup of tea.'

Robert filled Gemma in with all the details of the past few days and the general feeling amongst the local fishermen about the lack of warning of an incoming hurricane.

Gemma was a slim and very attractive blonde, well dressed with a beautiful speaking voice. Her main interest in her life before she met Robert was music. She could have been a professional pianist specialising in Chopin, but having gained a degree in chemistry at Stirling University at the same time as Robert was at Edinburgh University, she decided to work as a research chemist in a laboratory in Edinburgh. There she met Helen Spinks and eventually shared a flat with her in Queensferry. Helen was interested in outdoor activities, playing tennis whenever possible, but Gemma used her spare time either playing music or attending concerts, theatre or ballet.

It was one Saturday afternoon in June in a very busy Princes Street in Edinburgh, when Gemma was weaving in and out of the crowd of shoppers en-route for a closing down sale in a dress store in search of a black trouser suit for her nights at the concerts. Sifting through the racks of clothing she was suddenly confronted by Jackie Reynolds, a contemporary of Robert Watts and herself. This chance meeting of old schoolfriends was to change her life for ever. Jackie extended an invitation to her garden party, where she met Robert, and some eighteen months later married him.

Outside the landscape appeared bleak. The trees, laid bare of all foliage, stood without their summer mantle, producing a beautiful pattern against the sky.

Early mists robbed the countryside of all colour, reducing it to a series of greys. On occasions a thick fog would blanket out everything and deaden all sounds. The beginning of the long winter nights had arrived, with freezing temperatures, little sunlight and the threat of Christmas ever nearer.

Robert settled down to family life again, working against the clock with his lectures and writing, sometimes into the early hours. Grace Kennedy the cleaner was doing more than expected in keeping the household together and acting as nanny to the children. A twice weekly phone call to Mary on the island revealed no change in the situation. Alf Everitt called each morning on Mary bringing her fresh produce from his garden, she in return did some of his washing and ironing. As the days passed by, more sympathy letters arrived about the sad loss of Bert Watts. One particular letter of condolence from Jackie Reynolds offered help to Mary, for, as she put it in her letter, 'I only live down the road'.

It was about 2 pm on a grey November day. Both children were at school and the house seemed strangely quiet. Robert had arrived back from London by train and sat at his desk writing his notes. Gemma was stretched out on the settee reading a magazine ... The sound of the telephone ringing shattered the silence, and suddenly all life seemed to stop. There was a physical tearing at the heart.

Gemma nervously reached for the phone – the blood seemed to drain from her face as the voice on the other end started, 'This is the Northumberland police ...'

Robert had heard the phone and took the receiver from her hand. She stood away from him, watching the expression on his face.

Eventually he slowly replaced the receiver then turned to face her.

'Have they?'

'Yes I think so, they want me to identify ...' he said.

It was midday the following day after the phone call. Having driven through the night to Berwick mortuary, Robert mounted the steps to Jackie's house, straightening his tie, and rang the bell.

A look of utter surprise lit up Jackie's face as she opened the door and saw him standing there. 'Robert!' she blurted out. 'Oh how lovely, what a surprise, come in.' She led the way into a tastefully furnished lounge. 'Sit down. What brings you here so early?'

Robert sat in one of the chairs and leaned back, looking at the ceiling for a moment.

'I got a phone call yesterday from the police. A body has been washed up – they said it could be my father and want me to identify it.' He paused and looked at her, then continued, 'I have just come straight from the mortuary in Berwick.'

'And?' she asked.

'Beyond all doubt.'

'Oh God, you poor thing!' she exclaimed.

'They warned me before I went in that it might be a shock ...' He stopped, drew in a deep breath and carried on, 'It had been in the sea for a long time and was badly decomposed beyond recognition – parts were missing.'

She called out, 'Oh NO!'

'Jackie, this was the very first time I saw anyone dead belonging to me, my own father – what was left of him . . .'

'I'm so sorry Robert, it must be awful for you.'

'The dead have no resemblance to the living, he was not there in that room. My father whom I have loved was lying there before me and I just could not connect with him, not to this heap of something before me. Parts of his arm were missing, his face – well it just wasn't there. They brought in remains of his clothing and artifacts found on him . . . That is when I knew who it was – I recognised the multicoloured jumper mother knitted him about three years ago. It was torn and covered in plankton. His brown corduroy trousers with the black buckle belt and smaller items like his purse with the elastic band round it, his wristwatch with the chrome expanding wristband, stopped at 8.25, and finally his gold ring with the red garnet stone. Yes this WAS my father, what's left of him.'

'What a terrible ordeal for you – what happens next?'

'Oh the inquest, they will have to fix a date for that, then when they release the body I have to arrange a funeral'

'Does Mary know you've come north?'

'Gemma will have told her by now. I went straight to the mortuary. I don't know what the tide is doing?'

'I can put you up if you want to hang around. Roslin will be home about 5 pm, and John as you know is away.'

'Thanks Jackie, but I really should be with my mother at a time like this.'

'I understand, but if there is anything I can do, just ask.'

She left the room, leaving him with his thoughts. He stood up and walked over to the window looking out onto the patio. The four garden chairs were stacked up and covered for the winter, a few remaining flowers lingered on in their pots, reflecting on the damp stone tiles on the patio floor, nimbus clouds crossed the sky, it was a dismal dark day and the view did not do anything to elevate his thoughts.

After a while Jackie reappeared carrying a tray of coffee and biscuits and a tide table in her hand.

'There you are Robert, help yourself, and there is the tide table.'

'Thanks Jackie,' said Robert, picking up the tide table. 'Oh Lord,' he said, 'I can't get back until gone 4 o'clock in the dark.'

'Then you had better ring Mary and explain. In the meantime you had better get something to eat, I will take you to a bistro I know not far from here, what do you say?'

'Yes OK, that is fine.'

'In that case I will go and get ready – won't be long.' She almost danced out of the room leaving the fragrance of her perfume behind . . .

Over the meal Jackie did most of the talking, trying to keep Robert's mind away from his morning ordeal, knowing that he still had to tell his mother, while sparing her the more gruesome details. Occasionally their eyes met with the same intensity and desire they shared that day in the pub on the island. For a short while there was no world for them but that corner table on a cold day in November.

Robert arrived at 'Sea Winds' on Lindisfarne in the dark late afternoon. Mary threw her arms around him and cried. He had telephoned earlier so his presence was no surprise. Taking him into the lounge where a log fire was burning, throwing out a welcome heat, she sat down, eager to hear the news.

Robert chose his words carefully, explaining precisely the essential parts of his visit to the mortuary, leaving out the sinister and gruesome details. Mary listened with total concentration, hanging onto every word. At the conclusion she sat looking into the fire. The grandfather clock in the corner of the room reverberating its monotonous tick-tock seemed louder as the room fell into silence. Mary sobbed quietly.

After a while Robert broke the silence. 'There will be an inquest Mum, then they will release him for burial, until then there is nothing we can do.'

'No . . . I understand. Will you see to that?'

'Yes of course,' he replied. 'But I don't know how long it will take. That is something I will look into.'

'Oh what a mess, and Christmas coming up for you and the children.'

'Grace has agreed to look after the children when the funeral takes place.' He patted Butch's head as he lay in front of the fire . . .

A week passed by with no news of an inquest. Robert kept in touch with Gemma, who shared the same anxiety about the delays, with Christmas fast approaching.

'I think I will phone the police Mum, see if I can't liven things up.'

'You can try,' answered Mary.

33

Robert went to the phone. Mary collected the pots from the table and took them into the kitchen. Butch lay in his basket watching Robert's every move. The ever monotonous ticking of the clock was a constant reminder that life goes on.

After ten minutes or so Robert went into the kitchen to Mary. 'They say it really isn't in their hands, but in view of the fact that I have come some distance, they say they will try and speed thing up a bit.'

'Well, that is something I suppose. It could go on for weeks.'

He was no nearer a solution. If he stayed it could be weeks before anything happened. If he returned home he could find he had to come back immediately.

The clouds were breaking up, revealing more blue sky, and the wind had dropped to a mere whisper as Robert, with Butch, made his way to the harbour. It was no longer busy with police and newspapermen, just a couple of men working on repairs to their boats. How different everything looked now. The harbour a muddy dirty mess, birds scavenging for food and filling the air with their screaming. The absence of holidaymakers on this cold day made it strangely desolate.

It was late in the afternoon and getting dark when he arrived back at the cottage. Later that evening the phone rang and Robert's mind was made up. Grace the cleaner was ringing to tell him Gemma was in bed and the doctor had been called.

The journey back to 'Farcroft' in Leicestershire late in the afternoon on this November day was beginning to take its toll. The endless travelling north and south along the A1 no longer held the fascination it once had – it was becoming a chore, and there was more to come.

Street lights were on in the villages he passed along the road. In the distance cottages and houses glowed slightly amber amongst the fine mist of grey buildings and the fretted silhouette of roofs pointing upwards to a colourless sky drained of all tints and opacity with the coming of darkness. A half moon paled low above the treetops with no hint of stars – yet.

He turned his car into the drive of his home where it stood alone surrounded by fields and trees lit up like a Christmas tree. He recognised the doctor's car immediately, standing in the drive. Thankfully Grace was at hand to take care of things. Gemma greeted him with a weak smile as he entered the bedroom and was informed by the doctor that she had only just escaped pneumonia and must stay in bed for a few days. The last few weeks had been a great strain for both of them: the hurried meals, the long journeys, intermittent sleep, the anxiety and sight of his father in the mortuary. There was no let up for them.

The following morning was shrouded in fog. Lucky I came back yesterday – he thought. Grace had now been given time off, leaving Robert in complete charge. As nursemaid, child minder and housekeeper it left little time for him to write his notes for publication or prepare his lectures, forcing him to work into the early hours when the children were in bed.

It was ironic that it should take him into a mortuary for the first time to identify someone he loved, and to be told by those who counselled him before he went in, 'They look peaceful as if asleep.' Utter rubbish he thought, they are beyond reach, they are alone, remote like an unlit oil lamp. They are not beautiful, it's ugly, and a sudden death is a considerable blow to one's complacency, making you realise the extent you fritter away your emotional feelings on trivial matters – if only one had realised.

Days passed, Gemma's crisis was over and she was making good progress. Grace continued to stabilise the situation and with Christmas fast approaching, Robert would need all the help he could get. Then echoing through the house, sounding louder than usual, the telephone rang. Robert knew instantly with that gut feeling which comes when connected to someone emotionally, so he was quite prepared to hear an efficient and cold voice on the other end say, 'This is the Northumberland police . . .'

Putting down the receiver he stood as if rooted. Gemma called from the bedroom, 'Was that . . .?'

'Yes it was,' Robert replied. 'A week on Tuesday at Berwick Coroner's Office.'

FIVE

There had been rain during the night as Robert prepared for his long journey back north to Berwick. It was just after 4 am when he set off, leaving Gemma and his children in the care of Grace once more. This was the first week in December. He should be preparing for Christmas, arranging a Christmas party for his children and friends, acquiring a Christmas tree, shopping for presents and a host of other things associated with the festive season, instead he was on his way to an inquest on his father's death. His wife was just recovering from an illness and his own work was getting further and further neglected, with lecture cancellations up and down the country.

Dawn was breaking in the east as he sped towards Berwick. The rain during the night had made any threat of fog no longer a hazard. Arriving at about 10.30 am he stopped to ask directions. It was bitterly cold as he stepped out of the car, an easterly wind was blowing as he dodged the pools of rainwater in the car park. Turning up his anorak collar he made his way to the entrance of a red bricked Victorian building and mounted the steps into the warmth of the interior.

The entrance hall had a black and white patterned tiled floor. Old-style radiators stood along the walls emitting heat into the wide hallway with a wooden staircase leading off. The words 'Coroner's Office, First Floor' were displayed, pointing upwards.

He mounted the stairs slowly, arriving on the landing from which several brown painted doors led off. One door was slightly open, through which he could see several uniformed policemen and men in casuals standing around talking loudly. As he entered all eyes turned towards him and the conversation dropped suddenly as he made his way through them. The policewoman whom he had met previously stepped forward. 'You made it then? I'm so pleased.'

'Yes, I started out very early this morning.'

'You must feel very tired, are you going to be all right?'

'Feelings are mixed. I suppose I'll feel better when all this is over . . .'

'Yes it is a difficult time for you. It is not very pleasant when all the details are going to be brought back again. Just remember if there is ANY way I can help just ask, I'll give you my card before we go.'

'Thank you, you are very kind.'

She smiled at him and touched his arm.

'Take your seats please,' a voice sounded above the gentle murmuring. There were three rows of wooden chairs in the room, an old type wooden knee desk in the centre of one wall, and a double wooden cupboard in the corner. A smaller desk with a chair was situated under the window on which stood several large leather-bound books, no doubt of a legal nature. On the front of the desk was a collection of pens and pencils and a calendar. On the wall behind the big desk hung a picture of Her Majesty the Queen.

The police occupied the first row of chairs with Robert sitting next to the policewoman as he was the key person in the room. Members of the press sat in the row behind them. A small thin dark haired man carrying a pile of books under his arms was conducting the seating arrangements. Finally satisfying himself that all was correct he sat down at the small desk under the window. From his inside pocket he produced a pair of reading glasses, which he put on, and sat back.

Eventually a small, bald, clean-shaven, well built man in his early sixties entered the room wearing a beige suit. He nodded his greetings to the gathering as he walked in. Silence fell about the room as he sat down and put on a pair of rimless spectacles. The little man seated at the small desk handed him a pile of papers. One or two members of the audience coughed as they sat watching him go through the papers. Finally 'Good morning everyone' – he started looking around his audience. 'Normally we hold this type of meeting earlier in the day, but because the son of the deceased had a long distance to travel we delayed it. The inquest today is on the death of Herbert Watts, living on the island of Lindisfarne.' Robert felt a cold shiver go down his spine as he watched the coroner thumb through the papers.

'Herbert Watts was a very experienced seaman . . . He was born by the sea, worked on the sea and lived on the products of the sea. Before the Second World War after leaving school at 14 he worked for a small fishing fleet on the island as a crew member. The fleet at that time consisted of four trawlers working the North Sea for herring, mackerel, cod and whiting, The owner of the fleet was William Lathan who lived on the island. I must point out here that herring were in great demand at that time and were transported to Craster to a local kipper smoking firm owned by the Robson family. When war broke out in 1939 the fleet was dissolved, most of the men employed by William Lathan joining the Army or the Royal Navy. Herbert Watts joined the Merchant Navy. He was torpedoed twice, once in the Bay of Biscay, the second time in the Atlantic, where he spent three days in an open boat before being picked up by a British Frigate. I am telling you this to give you an insight into the kind of man Herbert Watts was . . .'

He stopped to take a sip of water from a glass tumbler on the desk.

'. . . When the war ended he returned to Lindisfarne and with his savings managed to buy a boat of his own from the fleet of William Lathan, who unfortunately never returned from the war. Herbert Watts became a well known and respected fisherman and member of the community on the island. He was very hard working, loyal and very experienced at sea. SO, what went wrong? You may well ask,' he said looking about the room. 'I am going to ask Chief Inspector Momson. Why did an experienced fisherman like Bert Watts go out in weather like that?'

The chair groaned as the inspector rose to his feet. He cleared his throat, then read from his notes held in his hand.

'About 10.30 am on the morning of 16th October 1987 I was informed by the local coastguard that a local fishing boat had been reported overdue from Lindisfarne harbour. Because of the very high tide that morning I was unable to get to the harbour until much later in the day. A very strong wind was blowing when I arrived, considerably less violent than earlier but still very rough. At the harbour I saw lots of debris lying about caused by the strong wind earlier in the day. Boats were damaged, wreckage was strewn about. One man came forward to tell me that the boat the *Northern Pride* belonging to Mr Watts was overdue. Mr Everitt who volunteered the information said he was the last person to see him go out that morning, and said that Mr Watts even joked about the weather. He said the time was just before 7.00 am when Herbert Watts boarded his boat and it was very breezy. Mr Everitt said to Mr Watts as he was casting off, "Mind you don't get blown away." He replied, "It will have to be a good one, Alf – it will blow the cobwebs away." Mr Everitt stood and watched Mr Watt's boat leave the harbour and go out to sea.'

'Thank you,' said the coroner, taking down notes before resuming. 'That was the reference Mr Watts made about the weather that morning.' He looked about the room above his glasses, then continued, 'I think we can establish the fact that a very strong wind was blowing – nothing unusual in that, but I have here a newspaper cutting which mentions a hurricane warning. WAS there a hurricane warning? Mr Zanker, would you please read out the weather report for that morning from the Met Office?'

Mr Zanker, the man sitting at the other desk, stood up, holding papers in his hand. Adjusting his spectacles he began in a low voice:

'The weather report issued by the Met Office for the day 16th October 1987 at 5.30 am predicted a deep depression over the Atlantic, moving in a north easterly direction and was developing ... At the time the report was given out on the radio and later on the television it was assumed the path of the depression would pass over the Spanish Coast and Southern France. There was no mention of a hurricane at this stage other than a very strong wind. However we now know to our regret that the depression DID develop and changed course veering northwards away from France and affecting southern England, particularly Kent and the town of Sevenoaks, then East Anglia, and out northwards into the North Sea where Mr Herbert Watts was fishing, with gusts of wind up to 95 mph.'

He cleared his throat.

'As the pressure and speed of the wind was not constant but fluctuated between 45 and 95 mph it was not classed as a hurricane, simply a very strong wind. It has been reported that considerable damage has been done to trees and property. Six of the seven oaks by the town of that name have been destroyed. 13 people have been killed, including firemen and fishermen. The more violent gusts were between 7.45 am and 8.30 am. I have here a comment from a national newspaper at that time ... A lady telephoned the BBC asking about a hurricane which had been forecast.' Mr Zanker looked up and shrugged his shoulders, then continued, 'As already stated the deep depression was being monitored out in the Atlantic and was set to miss our shores, but regrettably changed course.' He put the papers down on the desk in front of him saying, 'That, sir, is the weather report for that fateful day.'

'Thank you.' Silence followed as the coroner made notes. 'Constable MacKay , I understand you were on duty the day it was reported that wreckage had been found?'

PC MacKay stood up. 'Yes Sir I took the call, and when I realised the nature of the call I put it through to Inspector Goodwin.'

'Thank you, you may sit down. Inspector Goodwin, would you tell us exactly what the telephone call was about?'

Inspector Goodwin stood up, and Robert recognised him immediately as the officer who had taken him over to the boatyard. The policewoman sitting next Robert turned and asked, 'Are you all right?' Robert nodded and smiled weakly.

'At about 9 am on the morning of 6th November 1987 I was summoned to the telephone. A Mr Warmley, a marine engineer living along the coast towards Berwick, reported that a section of a boat had been sighted and brought ashore, did we think it was important?' He turned and looked at Robert before continuing.

'We thought it was important and arrangements were made to view it later that day.' He turned the page of his notebook. 'I then decided to take WPC Pemberton with me over to Lindisfarne to visit Dr Watts at about 10.15 am. Dr Watts is the son of Herbert Watts. We arrived at the cottage of Dr Watts, and when we told him the nature of our visit, he readily agreed to accompany us to view the wreckage.'

The coroner interrupted. 'You mean you went over to Lindisfarne?'

'Yes sir. The tide was low and we thought if he could identify the wreckage, we would be able to get him back home again before high tide.' He looked at the coroner.

'Carry on.'

'We picked Dr Watts up and took him to the boatyard owned by Mr Warmley. Dr Watts recognised the remains of his father's boat immediately.'

'Thank you, sit down.' The coroner made more notes then asked for Mr Warmley to stand.

Mr Warmley was a small thickset man in his early sixties. He had dressed himself in a shabby dark suit and white shirt with a frayed collar.

'Mr Warmley,' began the coroner, 'you claim you found the wreckage in question?' He nodded. 'Tell us in your own words exactly how you found it, please.'

Mr Warmley stood up rather nervously, 'It wa' about 2 o'clock I wa' just goin' to put boat in water for a test run, when I sees this thing in water about fifty yards out. What's that? I thought, so I started my boat and went to 'ave a look see. When I got near I could see it were off a boat. It had a name on it, so I thinks it must belong to some bloke, so I phone police like . . . an' me an' me mate pulled it ashore.'

'Did you think it was important at that time?'

'Dunno, it had name on it, must 'ave belonged to somebody!'

'When Dr Watts saw it and recognised it be his father's boat, what were his reactions? How did he feel about it?'

'He nearly passed out, 'ad to sit 'im on a box.'

'Thank you Mr Warmley, you may sit down' A slight ripple of movement went through the room.

'Now,' exclaimed the coroner, 'we have heard the evidence surrounding this awful tragedy of a brave man losing his life at sea. Mr Watts was born near the sea, worked on the sea and subsequently died in the sea. He was a man who no doubt would have great respect for the sea. On that fateful day, Mr Watts would have set out in the normal way, having first listened to the weather forecast before doing so. As he remarked to Mr Everitt, the last person to see him go off, it was a bit breezy, it will blow the cobwebs away. Had a day like that taken place during the last century, the mariners of the day would have welcomed it as meaning more wind in their sails. What happened out there that day in October was beyond the power of anyone to foresee, even with today's technology. The depression which was being monitored by the Met Office could not account for its change in direction. Unfortunately Mr Watts was caught up in it and lost his life.' He paused and looked over to where Robert was sitting with head bowed.

'In the second week in November the sea gave up your father's body and artifacts which you were able to identify in Berwick-on Tweed.' He looked in Robert's direction.

'Beyond all reasonable doubt that was your father?'

'Yes, that is correct.'

'Dr Watts, we all here today offer our condolences to you and your family and ask you not to put the blame on anyone.'

Robert nodded in agreement.

'I can record death by misadventure, and I will sign the necessary documents to that effect. Thank you ladies and gentlemen, that is all.'

The sound of moving chairs, muffled voices and shuffling feet filled the room. 'Dr Watts,' said the coroner, 'would you please stay behind?'

'May I offer you my own sincere sympathy.' The voice came from the policewoman standing beside him. 'I know it has been very hard for you

– perhaps we might meet again under more pleasant conditions – this is my card should you ever need me.' She held out her hand and shook his hand with a long hard handshake, smiled, then turned and walked towards the door, stopping only to wave to him before disappearing through it.

He stood looking at the empty space where she stood a moment ago.

'Mr Zanker will print off a death certificate for you and a release note so that you may proceed with your funeral arrangements.'

The coroner got up from his desk and came over to Robert, holding out his hand. 'From all accounts from what I have read your father was a very brave man. Serving his country and surviving the ruthless bombing of the German airforce is something to be proud of.' He placed his hand on Robert's shoulder. 'If it is any comfort to you, although you may not see it that way yet, he died where he loved to be – on the sea.'

Finally the clerk passed the papers over to him, 'You can now go ahead with your arrangements.' he said. 'The funeral director will advise you if you require further copies.'

Robert left the room thinking how matter-of-fact it all seemed, so unattached and unemotional. This was a human life going about his business as usual, until that unseen tragic crescendo swept him out on a dark tide. All through his life after the death of Linda in that Chinese earthquake he had known that even in the midst of happiness, the pain of life was always close by.

Robert walked towards the open door and descended the stairs. An employee was pinning a notice on the notice board in the entrance hall. Looking through the glass panelled doors he could see snowflakes falling. The vague figure of a female emerged from the corner of the half lit hallway and stepped towards him dressed in a long full length slim-fitting black coat and fur hat, with long black boots.

'Hello Robert, surprised to see me?'

'Good God Jackie, yes I am. What has brought you here?'

'I phoned Gemma only this morning to ask when the inquest was going to be, and she told me this morning, so I thought, I will go and meet him and see what the findings were, and also see if I can persuade him to have lunch with me as he cannot get back until late this afternoon.'

'Is that so?' he said holding her at arm's length. 'Not only are you very attractive but cunning also!'

Outside the warmth of the building they both felt the sudden change in the temperature. It was bitterly cold with snowflakes falling onto their shoulders as they clung to each other arm in arm. Passers by walked with umbrellas up or buried themselves in their coats. Traffic sloshed their way with lights on through pools of water where white snow had turned into brown, grey matter in the gutters.

Jackie almost danced along with Robert, hanging on to his arm and her face pressed against him. She led him off the main road down an alley which opened into a square and the warm welcome lights of a small restaurant. The pleasant smell of cooking met them as they entered. One or two tables were already occupied. Jackie moved towards a corner table and took off her coat and hat, then sat facing him.

'Was the inquest such an ordeal ?' she asked, taking his hand on the table with a squeeze.

'In a way yes, but not as bad as I thought it would be.'

The waiter approached with the menu.

'Good afternoon,' he said, with a strong accent.

'Good afternoon, Mario,' answered Jackie. 'Anything special?'

'Fritto Misto di Mare in the fish dishes or Orange Glazed Roast Lamb in the meat dish.'

'Mmmm, sounds appetising. What do you want Robert?'

'I think I will have the fish,' he replied.

'Me too Mario – thanks.'

The waiter left them to carry on with their conversation. More people came in, stamping their feet and shaking off the snow as they entered.

'Are you going to be all right in this weather, crossing over? I can put you up until morning if you prefer.'

'I think I will be OK. I have to see Ma and start making arrangements.' He half smiled at her. 'Besides, I would like to get it cleared up before Christmas.'

'You have a lot to do before then,' she replied.

'You can say that again! What about you? Is John coming home for Christmas?'

'You tell me,' she answered.

'As bad as that, then?'

'It is always like that, I never know when he is coming home, I sometimes wonder if I AM married.'

'The man is a fool. How could a man leave such an attractive wife for months on end – I couldn't. He is not cheating on you, is he?'

43

'How would I know, he is too far away for me to know.'

Robert shook his head and looked at her across the table. Her hairstyle framed a most beautiful face. Her eyes began to moisten, she lowered her head. He put his hand on the table, which she readily accepted. They remained like that until the waiter arrived with their order.

SIX

Eleven am in the second week of December, the day was cold with a temperature of minus one. A north east onshore wind was blowing from the North Sea. The island seemed strangely quiet and numbed as the hearse carrying Bert Watts came to a standstill outside his cottage 'Sea Winds'.

The tall figure of the undertaker dressed in black slowly alighted from the hearse and straightened himself, placed a tall black silk top hat on his head and walked sedately down the garden path carrying a silver topped walking stick.

Inside the cottage Mary, Gemma and Robert were already waiting, dressed entirely in black. Robert had decided that a second car was not necessary as the short distance to the church did not warrant it. By prior arrangement Butch, Bert's black Labrador, would also join the followers as a last respect for his master.

The tolling of the church bell sounded as the undertaker emerged from the cottage followed by the mourners. The cortege moved slowly, passing cottages with their blinds drawn as a mark of respect, their occupants joining the followers. Approaching the chapel Jackie, dressed in black, with her daughter Roslin, moved forward and joined the others, who now numbered about twenty villagers. It was a slow procession to the chapel which was already almost filled to capacity.

The vicar took over from the undertaker and headed the pall-bearers carrying the oak casket towards the altar. One solitary floral cross lay on top of the casket. The chapel on Lindisfarne was part of the ruined priory St Aidan had founded it in 635. Destroyed by the Danes in the 9th century, now only part of it remains.

The ceremony began with the hymn, 'For those in peril on the sea'. Robert read the lesson. Then the vicar from the pulpit recalled the life of Bert Watts.

The service over, the last notes of the organ reverberated around the church. The sound of muffled feet and the clanking of the oak door latch as the door opened let in a blast of cold air as the coffin of Bert Watts was carried outside to the open grave, his final resting place. Mary followed with Robert at her side, Gemma walked with Jackie and Roslin. At the graveside Jackie managed to stand close to Robert and during the few words and the Lord's prayer from the vicar, managed to find his hand and squeezed it gently.

There was little time left before the tide turned again after the reception. Some followers had already left. Jack Mason made it his business to have a quiet word with Robert. Gemma was in deep conversation with Jackie and Roslin. Gemma had already explained to her that she thought her children were a bit too young for a funeral, and she herself had driven up in her own car yesterday and was due to return tomorrow, leaving Robert behind for a few days with his mother.

Robert eventually left Jack Mason and returned to the cottage with Butch. Jackie was sitting on the settee with Roslin, Mary had disappeared upstairs and Gemma had put the kettle on. 'Well Robert,' said Jackie, 'it's finally over, now you can think of Christmas.'

'I don't feel very much like Christmas Jackie, I feel like escaping to some far off island for a week or two.'

'I know the feeling, I very often feel like that,' she said raising her eyebrows at him.

Outside cars were passing the cottage and people began to move again, the island was beginning to wake and become alive once more.

Jackie looked at the clock. 'Well, folks, I think I should be making tracks for home It all went very well today, and do keep in touch both of you, if ever you are this way give me a call.' She threw a quick glance at Robert. They both escorted her to the door. 'Goodbye Gemma, take care, you are very lucky,' said Jackie.

Robert held her tight. 'Drive carefully – see you sometime.'

Jackie's answer was lost in her emotions as she walked to her car parked outside the cottage. Gemma watched her get into the car, waved, then turned and went back inside the cottage. Robert stood looking at her as the car engine leapt into life. Jackie waved to him, then set off. He stood looking at the diminishing shape of her car, carrying away a woman who was becoming a part of his life. He wasn't sure how much or to what depth she had entered his life, he only knew it hurt. Falling in love is part of one's self and to have known love, though it be at arm's length and even for a little while, is more than some people realise in their entire life. And love, like roses has thorns.

There was an air of excitement running through the rooms of 'Farcroft'. The two children were helping Gemma to decorate the tall Christmas tree standing in the lounge.

Outside the countryside looked like a Christmas card, snow had covered the ground and filled the furrows in the ploughed fields, the tree lay bare and stark against the pale sky. Inside the house the heating was full on, Grace was busy cleaning the bedrooms and Sheba the house pet was asleep in her basket unconcerned at the level of noise around her. The whole house was vibrant.

Robert was trying desperately to catch up with his slides and lecture notes now that the funeral was over. In the quieter moments his thoughts turned to his mother, now alone on Lindisfarne. He had tried without success to persuade her to spend Christmas and the New Year with them, but her answer was,' I want to be with Bert this Christmas, I can visit the churchyard just before dark and stand with my thoughts.' Throughout Mary had put on a brave face, but inwardly she was grieving and openly crying in the privacy of her home. Butch was now her only comfort and companion. Outside her cottage the wind murmured, moving the curtains slightly. The grandfather clock in the corner stood proud with a steady tick-tock, the only indoor sound as she sat looking into the fire.

The postal delivery was later than usual, partly because of the weather conditions, but the little red van did make it in the lane approaching Bradgate Park. Gemma collected her delivery of morning post off the mat in the hallway. Along with the collection of bills and cards was a letter with unmistakable handwriting. Gemma recognised it immediately as coming from Jackie. Settling down on the settee she opened the letter:

Dear Gemma and Robert,

I will not be sending you the customary Christmas Card this year as I feel it inappropiate in view of your recent sad loss. I will however be thinking of you both, and of course Mary alone on Lindisfarne. She will no-doubt have her own thoughts and graphic memories at this time of year, I can only say again how terribly sorry I feel for you, it was a great shame. Bert will, I know, be greatly missed by his family and inhabitants on the island, which only time can heal. I may go over in the New Year to see Mary, I can then report back to you how she is coping. In the meantime if there is anything else I can do – just ask. Take care, all of you and

make the best Christmas you can for the children's sake. I'm not sure if John is
coming home, but I do hope so.
    Now Let us hope the New Year will be better for you.
    God bless
    Love Jackie.

Gemma put down the letter and walked over to the lounge window and stood looking at the white landscape outside. Jackie was a real friend, she thought, the type of friend you could rely and depend on. One you could trust with your life if needs be. She smiled to herself. Still clutching the letter she interrupted Robert at his desk, handed the letter to him then left the room.

The following morning saw a slight improvement in the weather. A weak sun was trying to break through the clouds, revealing a stark landscape of bare trees and hedgerows. Rooks' nests were now visible high in the tree tops and rabbits ran freely across the lawn.

    Robert had been summoned to London, a journey he could well do without. Although still cold outside one could now get about easily, though snow still lingered in the fields and hedgerows, a reminder of the last few days' arctic weather. A group of walkers dressed in variously coloured anoraks complete with walking sticks and back packs strolled past the house talking and laughing as they went. Gemma stood at the window watching them – they were a happy crowd, it was nearly Christmas and one should be happy, it is a time to celebrate, life must go on – but she knew it would take time for Mary and Robert to come to terms with that.

On this Christmas Eve Robert, now back from London, was waiting in the lounge for Gemma who was getting ready upstairs. The local school was performing a nativity play and Grace had offered to take the children, thereby giving them a chance for last minute shopping together. Eventually Gemma appeared wearing high knee length boots, a long black overcoat and matching Russian type fur hat. It was still very cold outside as they drove to their nearest town, Loughborough. Like all towns and cities on Christmas Eve, it was packed with shoppers going frantically about snapping up last minute bargains, clogging the doorways into the stores pushing and shoving. Cars threaded their way slowly through the masses of people carrying their burdens. Buses belched out sickly diesel fumes which hung in the still air. The smell of cooking sausages in hot fat, the aroma of ground coffee from the market stalls and the hot breath of people in a tight situation was getting unbearable and making it difficult to look in shop windows.

'Fancy a coffee?' suggested Gemma.

'Anything to get out of this!'

They entered a small doorway which yielded a flight of wooden stairs leading up to a coffee shop above a jewellers' shop.

'What a relief!' she said, taking off her coat and sitting down.

The afternoon light was fading fast as they came into view of 'Farcroft'. Grace had turned the outside lights on and the Christmas tree lit up shining through the windows made a welcome sight. Gemma presented Grace with her Christmas gift and Robert gave her a big cheque for all her help and work during the previous few weeks.

'Bath and early to bed tonight,' Gemma told the children. 'You know what day it is tomorrow don't you?'

This was followed with very big YES.

SEVEN

It was now two and a half years since Butch had died of cancer of the liver. This was a terrible loss to Mary, living on a remote island with her husband drowned at sea, and now her only companion also gone. Robert and Gemma spent two weeks each year with her since the death of Bert. Graham, Robert's son loved it on the island, he would spend hours fishing from the shore, and Zoe would spend most of her time horse riding with Jennifer Downing the daughter of the local sheep farmer. Now a more bitter blow was to be delivered. Mary had written to Gemma and Robert telling them that Alf Everitt had died after a short illness. It was six years since Bert was drowned, and since that fateful day Alf had been a regular visitor, bringing her fresh vegetables from his garden, she in return doing some of his washing. Now she really was alone.

Back home in Leicestershire Gemma was attending language classes at an evening institute. Graham attended martial art classes and played rugger in the school's junior team. Zoe was taking after her mother, learning to play the piano and horse riding at a nearby stable in Quorn. Robert meanwhile had been assigned to Austria by the British Museum in London to report on the discovery of a man found in the Austrian Alps believed to be 5,000 years old.

It was a clear Autumn night when Gemma walked outside into the garden. The sky was full of a thousand bright stars shining like diamond dust on a black velvet cloth as far as the eye could see. The planets Mars and Jupiter were clearly visible, and a faint breeze gently stirred the grass beneath her feet as she moved slowly around the flower beds. Looking back at the house, her thoughts went out to Mary, now finding herself alone on the island. She realised that one had to readjust to situations in order to survive. It must have been a shattering blow to Robert when his intended bride was killed in the Chinese earthquake He made the adjustment. Then again with the death of his father and the ordeal of identifying his body in the mortuary. It leaves a scar which you carry for the rest of your life. Now Mary was going through the same anguish and having to readjust. The loss of Bert, then Butch, now Alf, but she still remained defiant. 'This is my home, this is where I am staying.'

Gemma made her way back into the silent house, the children were in bed, Robert was away, everywhere was quiet. Sheba rose from her basket in the corner and followed into the lounge. 'What's the matter, Sheba? Don't you like being alone either?'

The telephone rang in the hallway. Gemma answered it.

'Hello Gemma,' came the unmistakable voice of Jackie. 'I have just been reading our local paper. Remember Kathy Stubbs at my garden party long ago, fat girl, good at netball, a bit bolshy, always had a chip on her shoulder. Well apparently her husband has been working in a garage – this happened last New Year's Eve apparently. He arrived home about six thirty and told Kathy he was going to get some drinks ready for the New Year before he settled down. There must be a superstore near to them – anyway, to cut a long story short, he never came back. He was knocked down by a car on his way back with his bottles. He died shortly afterwards.'

'Oh poor Kathy, I am sorry to hear that,' said Gemma.

'Well this is the report of the inquest which was held this week. A retired Army Major had been to a reunion and was driving back well over the permitted limit, when in a black spot with no lighting between Kathy's home and the stores, he veered off the road, hitting Kathy's husband. He was found guilty of careless driving but escaped a gaol sentence because he was 78, but was banned from driving for the rest of his life. He was ordered to pay costs and a substantial amount to Kathy's family.'

'What rotten luck. Poor girl, she has not had much luck with her life has she Jackie? First she gets pregnant at eighteen, now this.'

'I know. What about you, how are you keeping?'

'Oh I'm fine. Robert is away at the moment in Austria.'

'Then you are like me, Gemma, on your tod.'

'Yes, but my husband will be coming back. Anyway when the weather gets warmer you must come and stay with us for a few days.'

'I'd love that Gemma, thanks, that would be quite a change for me.'

'I can show you my part of the country. Well, thanks for telling me about Kathy, poor girl – keep in touch . . . Bye.'

* * *

Robert had been home for two days and sat at his desk writing. Gemma walked over to him and placing her hands on his shoulder, kissed him on the cheek.

'I've missed you,' she said.

'I've missed you too – when I'm away and lay on the bed in my hotel room, I wonder, what am I doing here? I should be with my wife and kids, not miles away. Then I think of the chaps in the services away from their loved ones for months on end . . .'

'True,' she replied, 'I suppose we are lucky really.'

He turned towards her and held both her hands. 'Do me a favour?'

'What sort of favour?'

'Play me something on the piano.'

'OK.' She moved over to the grand piano standing in the corner of the lounge. As if inspired she began to play with emotion Chopin's Nocturne No 5. The music filled every corner, capturing the mood of the countryside.

Robert stopped writing and watched her fingers move about the piano keys. The last chords were played – the room fell silent. Robert was clearly choked as he moved over to her. She turned to face him and lifted her head upwards towards him. He bent forward and kissed her with passion, she responded, clinging to him.

'Thank you darling, that was beautiful. You know you really should have gone professional.'

'No way. I was quite happy doing what I did in the labs. Maybe someone, somewhere has a new lease of life due to our research, I shall never know how many people throughout the world benefited because of our work. If I had gone professional I would only have affected a few, doing what I did affected many hundreds. The path I chose did more for humanity.'

He put his arms around her.

'Do you . . .?' she started.

'Yes very much.' He led her to the bedroom and closed the door.

Gemma lay close to him, their arms around each other, breathing deeply and feeling relaxed. Neither spoke. All had been said in the warming of one's body in unison, that which satisfies our deepest cravings, physical, mental and emotional, it does not matter what else life throws at us. This was the compensation for all the long periods of absence away from each other. Not to feel is not to live, and those who love are those who suffer.

They were both jolted back to reality by the sound of letters being pushed through the letterbox.

Gemma reluctantly released her hold on Robert who slipped out of bed and put on his dressing gown. The usual load of junk mail, Last chance reduction sale, Win a trip to Disney Land and a personal letter for Gemma.

Hurriedly she opened it. 'Robert, it's a letter from Helen, she has a daughter two weeks old and she has named her Monica after her favourite aunt.'

Waiting for the kettle to boil she read and re-read the letter several times, recalling the days they shared a flat together in Queensferry before either of them was married.

Four years later, Zoe was still taking riding lessons at the Quorn stables and winning rosettes at junior gymkhanas. Graham was now playing rugger every weekend as fly half. Robert was still commuting between London and Leicester. Grace Kennedy no longer cleaned for them now that the children were bigger, but would call round occasionally just for a chat.

Mary had been on her own now for over ten years since that fateful day in 1987. Robert and his family visited her every Easter, when Zoe would go horse riding and Graham continued his fishing, while Robert would go off looking for 'finds'.

No holiday would be complete if the four did not visit the Farne Islands, sailing from nearby Seahouses. They never failed to be thrilled by the sight of grey seals basking on the rocks and the hordes of various birds around them as they approached the lighthouse, made famous by the daring rescue by Grace Darling and her father the lighthouse-keeper in 1838.

After the trip, they would take a stroll along the coast's large expanse of sandy beach towards Bamburgh Castle, perched high on its dolerite rock known as Whin Sill, a huge sheet of hard rock stretching across from the North Pennines. Robert would pick up his usual stones and shells and explain to both his children their history.

Mary always made sure a good meal was ready on their return, listening to the exploits of her grandchildren.

EIGHT

Early summer flowers bloomed in the garden at 'Farcroft' beneath a clear blue cloudless sky. The midday meal over, Gemma sat in the conservatory engrossed in a novel. Somewhere in the distance a blackbird was in full song. Butterflies winged their way about the garden, bees passed from one flower to another in the search for nectar. The garden was alive with the sound of summer, and a nearby skylark rose into the air to add its chorus to the symphony. Gemma closed her eyes as she listened.

It was Zoe who returned home first to find her mother asleep in the conservatory. 'Excuse me mum, but I didn't know it was happy hour!'

'Mmmm – what? Oh hello Zoe, I must have dozed off!'

The sun was casting long shadows over the lawn, the chorus of birdsong had long finished. Gemma stretched herself. 'Oh, there is a letter for you on the hall table, there's one for your dad too.'

Zoe left to pick up her letter. She returned two minutes later holding the letter. 'They've accepted my application for the horse-trials! Mr Sedley says I can ride Ridge – he's a gorgeous jet black thoroughbred.' She threw her arms around Gemma's neck. 'Oh, Mum, I'm really happy now – "Gemma Watts on Ridge" – sound good!'

Have you ridden him before?'

'Oh yes, I've been riding him for weeks, we really understand each other, I talk to him and he knows what I mean.'

Good! We'll come and see you, of course.'

Graham came in dropping his baggage off in the hall then removed his shoes before joining the others in the lounge. 'Hi everyone, it's been a lovely day – what's new?'

Zoe filled him in with the details about the horse trials. 'That's great news. Wait till I tell my mates!'

Robert's car drew up on the gravel path outside. A minute later he was inside and already taking his anorak off. He moved over to Gemma and kissed her on the cheek. 'Had good day dear?'

'Nothing exciting, how's yours been?'

'Very good, actually.'

'Oh, there is letter for you on the hall table.'

'Right I'll get it,' and disappeared out of the room. Two minutes later her re-entered the room holding the brown envelope in one hand and the opened letter in the other. His face looked lifeless, all colour had gone, his eyes seemed fixed in a permanent gaze.

'Robert!' exclaimed Gemma, 'what is it?'

He hesitated, all eyes looked towards him. Holding out the letter to Gemma, he blurted out 'It's from the Leicester police – it's about Mary – she's had a stroke and is in hospital in Berwick.'

'Oh no!' was the chorus.

'I always thought something like this would happen. I'll give them a ring – see if I can find out exactly what did happen.' He left the room to silence, each one in their own thoughts.

Having driven through the night Robert arrived at the hospital in Berwick in the early hours of the day feeling stiff and tired. He made his way across the tarmac car park to the reception desk. After informing the receptionist the purpose of his visit he was told to take a seat and wait.

The waiting area in the hospital was alive with people, despite the early hour. Looking about him there were patients with an arm or a leg in plaster, some in wheelchairs, nurses in blue uniforms moved swiftly about, doors opened and closed with young-looking doctors and nurses carrying clipboards adding to this busy scene.

Robert became aware of a well dressed man in a dark suit talking to the receptionist. After a while the man turned away from the desk and walked over to him.

'Dr Watts?' he enquired, 'I'm Dr Mathews.' He held out his hand and shook Robert's hand. 'You have had quite a journey I hear?'

'Yes, as soon as I heard from the Leicester police I drove through the night.'

Dr Mathews was a small stout man in his late fifties with greying hair. They walked along the corridors until he stopped at a door with the doctor's name on it. Opening the door he led Robert into the light airy room overlooking the gardens outside. 'Do sit down, doctor, while I look for the papers.'

He withdrew from his desk drawer a large brown manila envelope. Sitting down in his chair, he pulled out a number of papers and began to thumb through them. Holding one in his hand he stopped and read its contents.

'Your mother,' he began, 'Mary Watts of Seawinds, Lindisfarne Island Northumberland was admitted to us on the tenth with a severe stroke.' He paused and looked at Robert. He continued, 'It was early evening, 7.15 pm to be precise. She was brought here by a Mr Mason, also of Lindisfarne. It is reported here that he drove through a foot of water to get her here in good time, had it been a little later there would have been no chance of getting her to hospital for several hours. Despite that heroic effort, the staff at this hospital put her on a life support machine and did everything possible to save her life. Unfortunately she died, never really regaining consciousness.' He looked a Robert. 'Dr Watts – had she lived she would have needed constant care. It was a very big attack and there was nothing anyone could do to save her.'

Robert sat looking at the carpet in silence, the blood drained from his face.

'I'm very sorry doctor. Her life gave out at 2.00 pm yesterday. I know it is a shock to you, but it was Mr Mason who remembered that you lived in Leicester but did not have your address or telephone number, so we put it out to the Leicester police.' He walked over to a cupboard. 'Can I get you a drink?' he asked.

Robert shook his head, 'No thanks.'

'Had you got here earlier there was nothing you could have done, and had she lived she would have been paralysed.'

This was the second time in his life he had to visit the mortuary to identify a parent. He turned back the white sheet covering his mother's body slowly, holding it tightly lest it slip back lower than decency permitted. Here lay Someone who had given him life and love, and now all life gone from her, alone and remote beyond the reach of civilisation, he stood looking down at her.

A sudden death like this and the one in which his father set sail one morning never to return made him realise how insensitive and blind and shocked we all are when we take for granted that they will always be there for us. What audacity to assume that there was life ahead when we arrange for the future: 'I'll see you tomorrow', or 'I'll ring you Wednesday'. Then the horror when there is no tomorrow. There was no tomorrow for his Linda who happily set off for China, there was no tomorrow for his father going about his work – his life taken by the sea. There was no tomorrow for his mother. One is left bewildered by all the little things which clutter up one's life, making us miss what was going on all the time around us – if only we had realised.

As if in a dream Robert left the mortuary, unshaven, pale and drawn, his eyes reddened through lack of sleep. He walked slowly along the corridor to the reception desk and made arrangements for the removal of his mother's body. He felt cold and tired. In a dazed state he turned to leave the hospital, instead he came face to face with Jackie Reynolds standing in his way.

'Hello Robert,' she said awkwardly with a smile, 'Gemma phoned me early this morning and told me you were in Berwick at the hospital. Have you eaten?'

'No, I've come straight from the mortuary.'

'She is dead then?'

'She died before I got here.'

'Then you are coming back with me.' She threaded her arm through his and led him out into the cool fresh air.

'You can get a day ticket from the machine and leave your car here – besides the tide is high at the moment.'

'But Jackie I . . .'

'No buts – you are in no state to drive, you look awful.'

She took him across the road to her car parked in a lay-by, neither speaking.

Jackie concentrated on the morning traffic in the short drive back to her home. In less than fifteen minutes they were in the house. Once inside she told him to remove his shoes and make himself comfortable.

'Egg, bacon and sausage all right for you?'

'Thanks Jackie you are very kind.'

'Nonsense, you look washed out. Get some food inside you then you can have a sleep before you start racing round making funeral arrangements.'

He filled her in with the details of how Jack Mason got her to the hospital, and the conversation with Dr Mathews.

'Oh Robert we shall all miss her, she was such a dear.'

Robert finished the meal she had prepared for him.

'Now Robert, I have to go out this morning, hair appointment, I should be back in about two hours. If you wish you can stay down here or go on one of the beds upstairs.'

'Thank you Jackie, I'll be all right.'

'Promise me you will get some sleep?'

'I promise,' he said with a smile.

She kissed him on the cheek and left the room, closing the door behind her.

It was midday when Jackie arrived back. Closing the front door quietly behind her she went first into the lounge where she had left him, then tiptoed up the stairs, to find him asleep on her bed. Smiling to herself she returned downstairs made a cup of coffee and settled down with the morning paper.

The whole house was quiet. Through the window trees and bushes moved gently in the wind, cumulus clouds had gathered, Jackie sat quietly reading, almost afraid to turn over a page lest the rustle of paper disturb her guest upstairs. Over an hour passed, when the silence was broken by Robert's coughing. Jackie sprang into action by going into the kitchen and brought the kettle back to the boil to make a cup of tea.

Opening the bedroom door slowly she stepped inside as he turned towards her.

'Had a good sleep? Cup of tea for you.'

'Thanks. What time is it?'

'Going on for one o'clock,' she replied.

'I must get moving.' He pulled himself upright in the bed.

'Hang on. We don't know what the tide is doing yet. I'll go downstairs and check.'

She returned with a tide table in her hand.

'The fourteenth – High tide at 10.45 am, 5.0 metres – so you cannot go just yet. Give it another hour or so then by the time you get to your car and the causeway you should be all right.'

'Jackie you are a real gem . . . thank you.' He emerged from the bed fully clothed and stood facing her then, taking her head in his hands, kissed her fully on the lips. They stayed like that for a moment then he released her, still looking into her eyes. 'Jackie, you are the most beautiful, wonderful woman I know. Thank you for everything.'

Jackie's heart was pounding, her eyes moistened as she held him tightly. 'Thank you Robert, You too are wonderful, I just like seeing you, and being with you.'

She let go of him and turned her gaze towards the window, hiding her tears. 'How long will you stay on the island?'

'I really don't know, there are a lot of things to sort out and I want to see Jack Mason and get his story.'

'Will you come back here? Or do you want me to come over to you?' she said, hoping for the right answer and turning round to look at him.

He moved slowly towards her, her mouth went dry as she stood looking into his eyes, searching for that answer he had left unanswered.

'Jackie you have already done enough for me.' He brushed a hair from her face and let his hand caress her cheek. For Jackie the world was about to stop, her heart beating – she let it happen, in a tight embrace they kissed with all the passion within themselves. After what seemed an eternity, they broke away slowly. A tear found its way down her cheek, he checked it with a finger. 'You are the most wonderful person I know. Thank you.'

The journey back to the hospital car park was in silence, both preoccupied with their own thoughts. The traffic was fairly light as she drove along, finally coming to a halt outside the hospital entrance. Robert turned towards her and took her hand.

'Jackie . . .' he started.

'No, please Robert, don't say anything,' she interrupted.

'I just wanted to say thank you for all you have done for me. Whatever I say is not adequate enough, I am proud and honoured to know such a beautiful, lovely woman. I have come very close to you. You are part of my life now . . .'

'Don't Robert please, just go – go – please Robert GO.'

Silence followed. Then he opened the car door and stepped out onto the pavement, while she drove off, leaving him standing there.

NINE

It was mid afternoon when Robert drew up outside his parents' cottage. He had done this journey so often, but this time it was different. He sat in his car looking at the cottage. Weeds had taken over the front part of the garden: bramble and convolvulus dominated, ragwort and broad dock leaves fought for space. His father's old pick-up truck still stood by the side of the cottage where he had left it years ago, now rusting, with lichen covering the roof and bonnet, the tyres long since deprived of air. This was once my home, he thought. Now with both parents gone it was just an empty shell.

He approached the door uneasily before inserting the key. The stale smell of cooking met him as he entered. The interior was uncannily silent, no-one to greet him, no dog to lick him, just the monotonous ticking of the clock in the corner of the room. On the table were the remains of Mary's last meal and a tumbler of milk.

He mounted the stairs to the bedroom. The bed was made, but Mary never made it that night. He moved to the other room and slowly pushed the door open. This was once his room. Still around the walls were shelves displaying his 'finds'. He moved over to the window and looked out at the castle on the mound. This is where it all started. What was going to happen now?

He went downstairs into the kitchen. Turning the tap on he discovered the immersion heater was still on, prompting him to wash the few pots Mary had left. Looking in the cupboards for foodstuff, he noticed a small tin box at the rear of one. Sitting at the table he opened the box. It contained insurance policies, bank books and statements. Birth certificates, some old photographs and view cards, items of jewelry and a photograph of himself in a Christening shawl, written on the back in pencil – 'Robert aged four months'. He sat motionless recalling happy memories as heavy footsteps outside approached the cottage followed by a knocking on the door.

He rose from the chair and answered the door. A red-faced stout woman stood before him, still wearing an apron. Her thick glasses framed a mop of grey hair.

''Ello,' she said with a smile. 'You don't know me.' To which Robert nodded an agreement. 'I live in Newcastle, but at the moment I'm staying with me brother and 'is wife, Mr and Mrs Belmont, round corner with green windows . . .' She hesitated a moment. 'I had just bin to visit me nephew's grave up in churchyard yonder and were on me way back before it got too dark, when I heard a knocking on window, I turned round an' saw a lady standing at your window, banging on it she was.'

'Is this my mother you are talking about?'

'Yes, I'm sorry I should 'ave said.'

'Then you had better come in.'

'Aye, that's window there,' she said pointing to the window. 'That's where she was standing just there.' She pointed. 'As I said she wa' bangin' on it real loud, so I went over to window, I think she wa' going to say summut but she just slipped down to floor, I didn't know what to do, I came in house and she wa' kicking and moanin' and breathing heavy like, so I ran out in road and went to first 'ouse I saw with lights on.' She paused and took a deep breath, then continued, 'The gentleman what lived there came back with me. He tried talking to 'er but she never answered. Then he said stay here I'll get my car and take her to hospital.'

'Would that be Mr Mason?'

'He was very good, 'e was, carried 'er out in 'is arms like a baby. I stood an' watched 'im drive off through water, 'e was very brave.'

'He certainly was, thank you for your part. I've only just got here, I was going to find out what exactly happened. Are you any relation to Jack Mason?'

'ME, oh no, never seen 'im before in me life. It wa' first 'ouse I saw wi' light on.' She had a kindly face. 'Would you be 'er son?'

'Yes I used to live here years ago. You are Mrs . . .?'

'Abbotson, Florrie Abbotson. It wa' quite scary. How is she?'

'She is dead. She was dead before I got here. It was a severe stroke.'

'Oh I am sorry, poor girl, very sorry.' She shook her head.

Robert had been on the island three days, on several occasions he had tried to contact Jack Mason. Together with making arrangements for the funeral, seeing his mother's bank manager and solicitor, the building society and the host of other things which need to be dealt with at the time of a death, had kept him busy, but amidst all that the haunting face of Jackie kept appearing, that look on her face when they stood close to each other, the smell of her perfume, the way her body yielded to him and the long lonely nights since, spent staring at the ceiling.

The temperature was only slightly higher than the previous day. As he opened the door of the cottage the cold seemed uninviting. The stone cottage had grown cold over the last few days. The uncertain date fixed for the funeral prevented him from phoning Gemma, and prompted him to light a fire and make the best of things.

Raking out the ashes from the previous fire was a chore he had forgotten about as his own life style had changed over the years. Placing the coals onto the newly lit fire he was sitting watching the flames licking the wood and coal when the telephone rang.

'Hi ya.' It was the unmistakable voice of Jackie. 'How are you coping?' His heart raced. 'I know you have a lot to do and wondered if you would like me to come over and give you a hand?'

'Hello Jackie,' he answered. 'Thanks for the offer but I seem to have done all I can for the moment, I am waiting to hear from the undertaker to give me a date.'

'Oh I see, so what are you doing now?'

'Just lit the fire, it is very cold in here. I spent the other day clearing up things in Seahouses, things like Mum's pension and a visit to the solicitor.'

'Want to come over for the day tomorrow?'

'Thanks Jackie, but I have got to refuse you this time.'

'Why? You have just said you have done all you can for the time being.'

'Yes I know, but I feel I should be on the spot just in case . . .'

'Robert,' she broke in, 'you're not afraid of me, are you? Look, John is away, as you know, as usual, Roslin is staying on at school extra activities then going on to her friend's house and won't be back till late. Why can't we meet just for a meal? I promise I won't eat you! Otherwise I shall have to celebrate my birthday on my own.'

'Your birthday – why didn't you say? That's different, of course we can meet. Where?'

Robert drew up outside Jackie's house about 11 am the next morning, mounted the steps leading to her front door two at a time and rang the bell.

She met him with a big hug and kiss.

'Happy birthday Jackie!'

'Thank you, dear Robert,' she answered.

'Now I must take you somewhere and buy you a present for your birthday then get back home just in case there is word from the undertaker, at least I shall know what to do then.'

'You just said back home, Robert.'

'I meant back to the island.'

Do you still regard it as your home?'

'In lots of ways, yes I do. It's always been there for me.'

'What happens after the funeral? Will you sell it or keep it?'

'I really don't know yet, but at the moment this is *your* birthday and I want to say thank you for all your help.'

'Thank you, you are so sweet. What I meant was if you sell, will we ever meet again?'

The time was spent visiting various shops and boutiques well into the afternoon. Both had now collected a number of large bags between them.

'Time we go back now,' said Jackie. 'We have a dinner to get to yet.'

They sat and talked over a cup of tea at Jackie's house, wrapping paper and cardboard boxes scattered about the floor. Jackie was making no excuses for her husband John.

'Sometimes I think there is Someone Else. I asked him but he denies it.'

''There must be something wrong with a man who could just go and live abroad leaving a very attractive woman behind. I couldn't. I know I go away a lot but I always come home to my family before too long.'

'Call it woman's intuition if you like, but there doesn't seem to be any spark any more. He never cuddles me. He is not interested in sex with me and takes no interest in Roslin at all.' Robert sat shaking his head. 'He is just dead wood. Anyway, tonight will be different. The taxi will be here at 7.30 . . .'

'Taxi!' he retorted.

'Yes, taxi. When we have had wine tonight you will not be in any state to drive. Your bed is made up in the spare room. Think of poor Kathy's husband.'

He watched her slim figure move across the floor, she was elegant, beautiful and intelligent. A warmth radiated from her, that look in her eyes smouldering then flashing like an animal watching its prey. She knew he was watching her and found no trace of guilt in her mind that he was happily married. She moved close to him as he rose from the settee. 'Robert,' she said, her lips almost touching his face, 'thank you darling for your birthday present.'

'My pleasure, glad you liked it,' he whispered slipping his hand around her waist.

She buried her lips in his in a long passionate kiss. 'You make me so happy.'

He sat watching the television while Jackie was upstairs getting ready, a cup of tea by his side.

The six o'clock news had finished as he heard her coming down the stairs. She entered the room looking radiant and stunningly beautiful. He almost stopped for breath. He stood up. 'Jackie you look devastating, absolutely gorgeous.'

'Thank you, that is nice.'

She moved towards him. He took her in his arms, they stood gently swaying. This is what she had been waiting for, the thrill of being wanted.

Dressed in a two piece beige suit, smart elegant shoes, her hair taken off her face and held at the back with a large ornamental comb, she moved towards the window and stood looking out, her perfume lingering as she moved . . .

Robert paid the taxi as Jackie stood on the pavement, then slipping her arm through his walked towards the door of the hotel and through the large swing doors. After checking in at the reception desk, they entered the restaurant area. Large chandeliers hung from the ceiling, wall lights ran the whole length of the room. On both sides of the room large full length mirrors set in white frames surrounded them as they walked in. A few people were already installed around the bar, some on stools others standing talking, laughing. After ordering drinks from the bar Jackie put her arm around Robert, more as a protective measure against the eyes of the male contingent who seemed spellbound at this beautiful woman and in some strange way craved her attention. She was aware of their attention and motives and disregarded them, turning her full attention to her companion. The conversation around the bar had dropped a couple of octaves for the next few minutes as heads turned from time to time with a weak smile.

Eventually the waiter directed them to their table; she could feel their eyes burning into her as she moved away, but she was with Robert and that was the way it was going to stay.

They were directed to a corner table.

'Will this do?' She asked him.

'Did you order a corner table?'

She smiled, 'We don't want to sit in the middle of the room with people round us looking at us, do we?'

'There is no stopping you, is there?' She did not answer.

The sound of a violin being tuned and the pianist adjusting his seat took Robert by surprise.

'I didn't know there was to be dancing – you never said it was a dinner dance?'

'Oh didn't I? Sorry, I must have forgotten.'

'You know you didn't. First the taxi, the hotel, then the corner table, now the band, what's your Plan?'

'Plan!' she answered quickly, 'there is no plan, only it is my birthday.'

'You have trapped me Jackie, and you know it.'

'Robert dear, there is no trap – you are free to go whenever you wish.' She smiled at him as she held his hand over the table.

The music started with a quickstep as they ate their first course. Four or five couples danced under the watchful eyes of the diners.

Robert refilled her wineglass, and she smiled at him as he raised his glass to her.

'When was the last time you danced?' she asked.

'Phew! I don't really know Jackie . . . years. How about you?'

'Same. It was certainly before John went abroad.'

'Do you feel like dancing tonight?' The question was asked as she took a sip of wine.

'I suppose so, if it fits into your plan.'

'There is NO plan!' She stood up and held out her hand to him. 'Come on dance with me, fall into my trap,' she laughed.

He held her close as they moved to the rhythm of the music, their cheeks touching. Two people together – their emotions and feelings for each other were now entering a new level. Her perfume excited him, a strange feeling of enlightenment gripped him as he turned her round in the spins on the floor. Jackie was in the mood, exalted and not wanting the music to stop. This was a moment of triumph for her, alone at last with her Robert.

Finally the music stopped, the dancers applauded and left the area. What was a moment or two was an eternity to Jackie, as they both stood there holding each other, gazing into each other's eyes, before leaving the floor.

Robert filled her glass again and passed it to her. She reached to take it, holding his hand around the glass. 'Thank you dear, that was terrific.'

The evening moved on, the third bottle of wine now half empty as they sat looking at each other. Something had happened in their world tonight, maybe for the first time in their lives. Perhaps all lovers think that, had they have both discovered the true meaning of love?

Throughout the rest of the evening they drank wine, talked, and danced until finally the last waltz was announced.

'Good heavens, is it that time already?'

'Yes Robert it is, and thank you for making my birthday a really happy one.' She rose from her seat. 'I feel somehow when the music stops tonight and the clock strikes twelve I shall return into rags and my Prince will have gone.'

'You will never return into rags, tonight you are the most beautiful woman in the room.'

The last waltz came to a close, she held him close to her. 'I love you Robert, very much.'

He stood apart from her, a tear trickled down her cheek. 'I love you too Jackie, I can't help myself.'

On the way back home there was no sign of a let-up in Jackie's onslaught. She threw herself at him, leaning hard against him, kissing his ears, his mouth, his face, all he could do was hold her.

Robert paid the taxi outside her house. Mounting the few steps leading to her front door was an achievement for her, her legs were not responding as they might. Once inside she swung round to face him and held him in a tight embrace before going into the lounge. On the table was a pile of books and a scarf on the chair back, a sign that Roslin had returned home and gone to bed. Swaying slightly she said, 'I'll just go up and see if she is all right.'

Robert sat on the settee, his head thrown back looking at the ceiling.

Jackie reappeared. 'She is fast asleep – fancy a nightcap?'

'God Jackie haven't you had enough?'

'NO – I want one anyway, I'm having a vodka, can I pour you something?'

'Just a very small whisky, please.'

'This has been the most wonderful night, Robert, for me for a very long time. Thank you darling. God if you only knew exactly how I feel, there are no words to describe them, all know is I am in love with you.'

They sat on the settee together, both bolding a glass, then with an abrupt swift movement she raised her glass high and said, 'To us and love.'

'Jackie,' he began, 'I'm already spoken for, as much as I love you I will never leave Gemma.'

'Darling I wouldn't want you to. All I want is a little part of your time, I have no-one.'

Silence fell about the room. The wind rustled the leaves on the bushes outside on the patio. He turned towards her and kissed a tear running down her cheek.

It was after 1 o'clock and the events of the long day were having an effect on him. Keeping his eyes open was proving difficult. She rose from the settee, making an excuse to leave the room. He sat motionless, deep in thought. He knew she wanted him as much as he wanted her, but deep inside him something was clouding the issue. He had to find a way to prevent the inevitable happening. He was on the brink of cheating on his wife. The effects of the drinks and the smell of her perfume sent his mind into turmoil, obliterating the responsibility of his marriage. His eyes became heavy through tiredness as he closed them from time to time, denying his body the sleep it required.

He was brought back to reality like a bomb exploding. He sat bolt upright as Jackie entered the room wearing a see-through nightdress with a flimsy loose gown over it.

'Jackie what . . .?' She held a finger to her lips and sat down beside him. He could see her pink flesh through the material, her rounded breasts and proud nipples.

'Jackie, please don't do this to me.'

'What is wrong love? Don't you want me?'

He stood up 'No Jackie, I can't. Forgive me but it has been a very long day for me and I am tired.'

He was wide awake early the next morning after a restless night. The sun was shining through the chintz curtains. He was aware of voices coming from downstairs and the clatter of plates. He lay still looking up at the ceiling thinking of the events of the previous night, in many ways resenting the fact that he had not made love to her, how would that affect their relationship now? She was beautiful, intelligent, fashionable, and she loved him. What now?

* * *

67

The voices downstairs grew louder as they moved into the hallway. Then a much louder voice, 'Bye Mum.'

'Bye darling, see you tonight.'

He heard the door close, then silence. The clock by the bed said 8.15 am.

A muffled sound outside his door made him alert and turn his head towards it. A gentle knock on the door followed by the door being slowly opened followed by Jackie, still in her nightdress and wrap, carrying a cup of tea.

'Good morning darling, cup of tea for you. Sleep all right?' she asked, putting the teacup on the bedside table and bending over to kiss him.

'Sort of,' he answered. 'Did you?'

'Yes and no – that was Roslin going off to college . . . Can I get in with you for a cuddle?'

Taken by surprise and before he could give an answer, she drew back the bedclothes and was lying beside him.

'Put your arms around me darling – please.' He turned towards her. The closeness of her body against him, the feeling of her nightdress against his own flesh aroused him. She drew herself even closer to him, feeling him throbbing against her. She pushed herself to him and kissed him. Her mouth went dry as his hand brushed her breasts and nipples, her body moved and writhed in response, she uttered a soft cry. 'I love you,' she whispered.

'I love you too, Jackie.'

'Don't stop darling, not now.'

Sliding his hand down her thigh she uttered a sound and offered herself to him, her body was vibrant, responding to every touch he made. She kissed him long and hard as she felt him enter her, thrusting. Her body rose and fell with every move he made. Her mouth was wide open as she gasped for breath. Their bodies worked in perfect unison as she felt a climax about to happen.

The pace quickened as he thrust even deeper, until finally she cried out as her body convulsed receiving his final thrust.

TEN

Banks of cumulus cloud were building up on the horizon leaving large gaps of pale blue sky against which seagulls cried and wheeled around in circles, occasionally falling like a stone into the sea and re-appearing again with a catch in its beak.

Robert walked down the garden path of 'Sea Winds', now overgrown with weeds and tall grasses. Only a small area had been cultivated by Mary since Bert had died, sufficient for her needs, the rest of the garden had been allowed to run wild. Along the boundary fence were rotting wooden pallets, crab pots, yards of netting and ropes, corks, marker buoys and anchors. Amongst the tangled weeds and boxes half hidden by tall grass was the remains of his father's boat *Northern Pride* that he had rescued from the boat builder. Now lying exposed to the weather, its once white paint peeling off and the nameplate barely visible, he stopped in his tracks and stood looking at this memorial to his father, this reminder of all that was left of the man who brought him into the world, served his country and worked hard all his life – this was his trophy. He turned to go, when through the tall grass next to the boat remains he saw a rough wooden cross. Clearing a path through he stopped, and saw there roughly painted on the cross a single word: 'Butch'.

Kneeling down beside the cross he reached out his hand and touched it. Memories of happier times flooded back to him.

'Hello there!' came a voice from the road, bringing him back from his silent prayer. The voice belonged to Jack Mason, standing at the garden gate.

'Hello Jack, I've been wanting to see you.'

'Sorry to hear about your mother.'

'I have to thank you Jack for the gallant effort you made and all you did for her. I've looked every where for you.'

'I've had a few days in Edinburgh with my brother.'

'Well thank you so much, Jack.'

'I had just finished my tea when there was loud banging on the door, nearly brought the door down, then a woman's voice shouting, QUICK, QUICK – she nearly made me choke.'

'That was Mrs Abbotson.'

'Aye she was right distraught, almost hysterical. At first I could not make out what she was saying, but I guessed it was something serious, so I just followed her. When I saw your mother I knew I had to do something fast. No use phoning for the ambulance, so I decided to take a chance on the tide – just made it.'

'Thank you Jack. She was dead when I arrived you know.'

'I'm very sorry, it must have been quite a shock but I wasn't surprised when I saw the state she was in.' He shook his head. 'My wife phoned the hospital so they were ready for us.'

'I do appreciate it, you were very brave.'

'When is the funeral?'

'That is what I am waiting for.'

'It's some time now since your dad died isn't it?'

'Yes, Mum put a brave face on but inwardly she was lonely, with Alf going as well.'

'So what happens now when everything is settled, do you sell this place or keep it?'

'Don't know yet, I haven't decided.' Robert turned and looked at the cottage.

'Keep it then if you can afford to use it for your holidays, it is your sanctuary, it belongs to the village not the weekenders. You were born here, this is your place, your home, your escape. Think about it. Think about it and be like Saint Aidan – use it to get away from the mad world.'

'I'll do that Jack, when I have sorted myself out.'

'You do that. I'm off to the pub, fancy joining me?'

'Not this time, I've got to wait for the undertaker – some other time.'

'Sure, when it is all over eh!'

Robert watched him walk smartly along the road to the pub. Thanks Jack. This could be his sanctuary.

It was afternoon, and Robert was sitting quietly in the chair pondering over Jack's remarks. The tick-tock of the grandfather clock was the only reminder that life goes on. The telephone rang shattering the silence, making him jump. He knew instinctively who the caller was. The long awaited call arrived, setting things in motion. The funeral was fixed for Friday of the following week at 1.00 pm.

He telephoned Gemma with the news, giving her a list of things he would need as it was pointless going back to Charnwood only to return a few days later.

He looked out of the window. People moved about their business as usual, some walked, others on cycles, occasionally a car passed, life went on. Now the final act was about to take place, then he could relax, and where better to relax than the beach?

He was leaving footprints in the wet sand as he walked along the sea's edge of a receding tide. The sea, a green-blue colour, was heaving as if reluctant to leave the shore, throwing spume high into the air. The fresh breeze ruffled his hair as he walked head down looking for 'finds' – a lifetime habit.

Out on the sea a small fishing boat moved up and down on the swell. He stopped and looked. The boat had cut engine and moved at the mercy of the waves. From the distance he could just make out the figure of a man busy preparing crab pots on a shank to be lowered into the sea. That could be my father, he thought. Ragged nimbus clouds dragged across the sky as he watched the figure finally lower the pots overboard, with marker buoys riding the waves. The sound of its engines re-starting as the boat moved on left him standing as if rooted to the spot, with past memories of a lost loved one. His father had done this type of work all his life in all kinds of weather. It was a hard life and not well paid, but Bert loved the sea, it is where he belonged. In a way he thought it apt that he should lose his life in the sea, isn't that what the coroner said?

He continued to walk along the high tide mark, occasionally stooping to pick up an object for inspection, examine it, then either put it in his canvas bag or discard it altogether. Bladder Wrack, Notched Wrack, Sea Mat lay about. Some rolled about in the wind with Whelk Egg Cases, Razor Shells and Scallop Shells beneath his feet, cracking as he trod on them. Pieces of twisted tree branches and driftwood probably from some far off shore. Bottles and cans carelessly thrown overboard from some seagoing vessel littering the beach. His beach.

He had been walking for over an hour before finally turning away from the sea on his way back to the cottage. He felt much better within himself now that final arrangements could be made. He took in gulps of fresh air as he turned and saw the castle perched high on the rock in the distance. He smiled to himself. His head now cleared of everything that had cluttered up his thinking was now resolved. The cottage was his now and he was going to keep it, this was his sanctuary.

The following morning was moist and warm. A pale mist hung in the far distance. The fragrance of the damp earth wrapped itself around him as he walked through the front gate of the cottage whose address he had been given to fix up the hire of the village hall.

Jackie had agreed to look after the catering when she knew the number of people attending the funeral. In the past Mary had undertaken this duty for Bert, then, Sally – Alf's wife, then Alf himself.

Having booked the hall for Friday afternoon he made his way back to *his* cottage, now looking sad and lonely like an empty shell. Gemma and the two children were miles away, so too was Jackie who had come into his life in a big way. He was tired after a gruelling two days. The thought of Jackie constantly in his mind took him into bouts of depression then into one of joy and happiness. New sensations with soft beautiful words are locked away in one's memory where no-one else has access. People should be happy, but under certain conditions those moments of happiness only last for a brief time. Values are falsified in the complexities of civilisation. Why do we allow ourselves to get emotionally involved to such an extent that it gets out of control? There are voices within us showing us the way to paradise but we cannot or do not want to hear. Peace and sanity will creep back into one's life after a time, but what sort of price do we pay?

When he set out for Berwick a week ago, he had only one thing on his mind – his mother. Unfortunately she died before he got to her. Now with a funeral to organise his own married life had been put on hold. That he could cope with, but Jackie was a different matter. It was unexpected, leaving his mind in turmoil like a cancer eating away at him, haunting him wherever he went. He walked to the window and stood looking out. Jack Mason was on his way for his pint at the pub. In a flash he was out of the door to join him as if chased by a demon.

'Jack,' he shouted, 'are you going to the pub?'

'Yes. Coming with me?'

It was afternoon when he arrived back at the cottage. The temperature had risen slightly with a few puffs of white clouds against a blue sky.

Opening the front gate into the path, the smell of damp earth still lingered. He stood for a moment looking at the untidy mess, shook his head and went indoors.

He was preparing a snack in the kitchen when the phone rang. It was Jackie. 'Robert, have you got the numbers yet?'

'Yes Jackie I have, I estimate 50 to 60 people.'

'That is fine, now I can tell them. How are you coping?'

'Not too bad, killing time mostly. I feel better now that I have hired the hall.'

'I know darling, it has been a drag for you. I miss you.'

Those words were like a dagger to him. 'I miss you too, I keep thinking about you.'

'You must not, you have things to do to keep you busy. Same as me. Bye Robert. Take care.'

She hung up, leaving him standing there still holding the receiver, as if turned into stone, before he could say anymore.

He finished his snack, washed the few pots left over from breakfast, cleaned out the ashes from the fireplace, then went upstairs to the bathroom and washed.

A light breeze had sprung up, ruffling the bushes and grass as he walked through the gate and turned left towards the harbour.

Seagulls screaming and wheeling around meant only one thing, the fishing boats had returned with their catch . . .

As he walked along the quayside Robert acknowledged the occasional nod from the fishermen working on their catch, re-coiling ropes, cleaning down the decks and the host of jobs at the end of any day's fishing. Weaving his way through the pile of boxes stacked high with fish, or crabs, he was suddenly confronted by a very stout man with full black beard wearing a stained blue jersey. He stood squarely in his path with arms folded revealing tattoos which ran the whole length of his arms. 'Hi', he said grinning. His irregular teeth stained yellow with smoking became the focus of Robert's gaze. 'They tell me ya old man wa' a crabber.'

'Yes, that is correct.' Robert replied.

'Did 'e 'ave a contract wi' Craster?'

'I believe so, why?'

'I've been made redundant wi' brewery I worked for, so started to do a bit of fishing like, thought you might 'ave sum gear to sell?'

'I don't know about to sell you, but if you would like to bring your truck or lorry or whatever, you can take the lot away, crab pots, netting, anchors, the lot, even the old pick-up truck if it's of any use to you.'

'How much?'

'Nothing – just take it'

'Aye, you're a bloody pal! When can I come?'

'I have a funeral on Friday, my mother's, so I don't want you there then.'

'Ya mean ya just lost you mum as well. Fuckin' hell, ya poor bleeder, both of 'em gone now then?'

'Yes . . . Oh, just one thing, at the bottom of the garden is part of an old boat with the name Northern Pride painted on it, and next to it is a wooden cross with the name Butch painted on. I don't want those touching, please.'

A large rough hand was held out as a final thank you, his grip of iron almost making Robert wince as his was shaken vigorously.

He arrived back at the cottage and sat in the chair letting the silence of the room wrap itself around him. Just three days to go before the funeral. He closed his eyes and fell asleep.

The light of day had diminished considerably when he opened his eyes. A cold chill ran down his spine as he looked into an open unlit fireplace. Switching on a light, the big clock in the corner showed 5.20 pm. He stood at the back door looking down the garden at the tangled mass of weeds and fishing gear. A half moon was already visible rising low over the sea and a solitary planet was shining. He could hear the sea breaking on the shore in the distance. Walking out into the cool air he stood looking down at the remains of his father's boat and the cross with Butch's name on it. On Friday, he thought, Mary will join her husband.

He woke early the next morning after a restless night and looked out to a blue sky with little white clouds dotted about. Normally he would have said this was a beautiful morning, but today his mind was in complete turmoil. The funeral in two days' time had taken up most of his thoughts. Arrangements had been made for the grave of his father to be opened up to accommodate Mary. The florist had been dealt with, the vicar, the hall, the refreshments and now a man coming to take away all Bert's old equipment in the hope of restoring some kind of order to this jungle of weeds and rusting fishing gear. Once it was all out of the way, the thought of Jackie reappeared, in his agony of regret. The very image in his mind of her – her perfume, the way she looked at him, her trim figure and everything about her tormented him constantly, relentlessly.

He washed and shaved, dressed and made himself toast, switched on the radio and listened to the morning news. Outside the noise of traffic moving away from the harbour suggested the tide was low and yesterday's catch was now en-route for market.

The air was full of screeching seagulls swooping and diving for scraps of food left behind by the fishermen as he opened the door of the cottage and walked down the garden path. With time on his hands now until the funeral he decided to make a start on getting the garden tidied up in readiness for big Jim to collect and take away.

Being unaccustomed to this type of work it soon began to have an effect on him. He was hot and sweaty, his hands covered in dirt and grease as he threw tarred rope, old tyres and smelly crab pots in a heap ready for collection. He was into this back-breaking operation over an hour when he heard, 'Hi there!'

It was Jackie Reynolds dressed in three-quarter length tight-fitting knee trousers, a light coloured cardigan, and looking as elegant as ever.

'Hello!' he said, letting everything drop from his hands and stepping towards her. She almost ran the last few steps to him, throwing her arms around him and tilting her head as she kissed him.

'I just had to come Robert darling. Gemma rang me last night and told me she was coming tomorrow with the children, and then I had a most horrible thought. When the funeral is over you will all be going back to your home, and God knows when I shall see you again.'

'I'm so glad you have come, Jackie. I've done nothing but think of you since I came back here. Let me go and wash and change into something clean, my hands are filthy.'

They walked back into the cottage, feeling the difference in the temperature as they entered. Robert disappeared into the bathroom, Jackie sat on the settee and picked up a magazine left by Mary. Ten minutes had passed when he entered the room cleaned and changed, and she immediately put down the magazine and flung her arms around his neck.

'The other night when we were on the phone, I just had to ring off darling, I was so emotional, I could not help it.'

'I know – I'm going through the same distress, I miss you,' he said, kissing her on the forehead.

'At least we have today together, so let's make the most of it.'

'OK, let us start with a walk along the beach instead of the harbour.'

'I would like that, you can tell me what to look for.'

'What are you looking for, Jackie?'

'Love Robert, love, I'm looking for real love, not marriage to some man a thousand miles away. He is a complete stranger to me when he does come home.'

'Jackie I can only give you a very small part of me. I have already let Gemma down, I know it was wrong, yet somehow in my confused mind it did not seem wrong, and it still does not.'

'I love you so much, that is why I am here today – I just had to see you. In about four hours time the tide will be in and I shall be gone. Do you know what that means to me?'

'Yes I do,' he said, hanging his head down. A stony silence hung about the room, both standing with their own thoughts. Just the ticking of the big clock and the occasional barking of a dog somewhere in the distance. He turned slowly towards her and took her in his arms, kissing her passionately. 'I'm torn apart Jackie, I love you so much, I know it is hard for you but it is equally hard for me.'

'I know darling. The other morning when Roslin had gone to college, what happened was the most beautiful thing in the world for me, I have NO regrets.'

'Me too, that was very special.' She kissed him.

'Come, let's go for that walk.'

Walking along the sea's edge their arms around each other, Jackie's head resting on his arm, both were in their own private world. The tide was well out, leaving a vast expanse of wet sand. The sun was warm on their backs, gulls circled around against the blue sky, in the distance the castle on the rock beckoned them, sheep grazed on its slopes, a few people had ventured the long walk and were rewarded with a beautiful panoramic view of the island. On the beach a few dog walkers strolled along, their dogs chasing the gulls in a futile attempt to catch them, but for two people so in love, they could have been on a tropical island in the Pacific.

They had walked for over an hour. 'Can we go back now?' she said.

'Of course, if you want to.'

'It is so peaceful and clean here, no diesel fumes no grime, no wonder you love it here.'

'This is my sanctuary Jackie. There is no other place like it. I came here for a month when Linda lost her life in China – I just had to get away.'

Back at the cottage Robert made a pot of tea and sat with Jackie on the settee.

'We have less than two hours left then it is the big goodbye, 'Jackie said sipping her tea.

'I'll see you on Friday at the funeral.'

'I know, but we will not be together.' She turned towards him. 'You will try and see me again, won't you?'

'Whenever I can, but it is not going to be easy now that both my parents have gone.' He touched her face.

She turned and kissed his hand. 'Make love to me darling, please.'

He led the way upstairs to his old room.

'Gosh! Is this all your doing?' she said, looking about the room at the many shelves displaying shells, rocks, charts and photographs.

'Yes, they go back years to when I was living here, but during term time I lived with my aunt on the mainland.'

'If only I had known then what I know now,' she said, putting her arm around him. 'Which is your favourite piece?'

'Oh that has to be this one,' he said, pointing. 'I was late for school one morning when I was living with my aunt and in the wall alongside the road I discovered this – it's an ammonite, I was so thrilled I forgot the time. Jackie you are looking at something which is over sixty million years old.'

'Good lord!'

'I also found these on the beach after a very rough sea – two Roman coins.'

'Don't say anymore darling, please, you are making me love you more!'

'Sorry!' he said, sitting on the bed beside her.

She pulled him down towards her and kissed him passionately.

They lay together with their arms entwined around each other, both breathless after the exertion.

Neither spoke. She had satisfied his deepest cravings, could he ever feel the same towards Gemma. Again he questioned himself. His emotions were divided. He longed to see his children again, but now Jackie was well and truly in his life.

He lay beside her naked beautiful body. She kissed him gently as she ran her fingers along his chest, he had found completeness, but at what price? When your innermost nature is satisfied physically, mentally and emotionally and at peace, without which everything is rendered futile, it does not matter what else life throws at you.

Outside the noise of gulls started. Robert looked at his wristwatch. The tide had turned. In their passionate moments they had forgotten the real world, carried away to some dreamlike existence.

'The tide, Jackie!' he said, almost in a panic, 'It is getting late!' He leapt out of bed to look through the window. Jackie lay there laughing.

'What is wrong?' he asked turning towards her.

'YOU! Look at the male beautiful, what a beautiful body you have.'

He realised he was completely nude. He turned quickly towards the bed and withdrew the bedcovers from her revealing her own nudity.

'Not nearly as beautiful as yours.'

The following morning was overcast. Large cumulus clouds occupied most of the sky, beneath them nimbus clouds moved swiftly.

Floral tributes from the neighbours were already arriving at the door of the cottage. Gemma had phoned him to say they were about to set off and would arrive late afternoon. Jackie had also phoned, and the conversation they had was to torment him all day. Sympathy cards were pushed through the letter-box, these he displayed on the shelf above the fireplace. He realised the next five hours or so were going to be difficult for him.

He lunched at the pub. His presence was always congenial, the locals showing him great respect and offering help if needed. The afternoon was spent around the harbour watching the activity and generally wasting time until his family arrived.

Around 6.30 pm Gemma arrived at the cottage with the children, looking hot and tired after the long drive. He had prepared a salad tea for them already on the table. The children were excited telling him of their recent exploits. Zoe had won a silver cup and rosette in the junior section in the local gymkhana, and Graham was making good progress with his jujitsu. By nine o'clock the two children were off to bed, leaving Robert and Gemma alone to talk about the funeral arrangements. By ten thirty Gemma retired for the night, feeling very tired after her journey, leaving Robert to himself and his thoughts.

He sat reading the newspaper for some time before finally calling it a day. Gemma was already asleep when he entered the room quietly. Having undressed he slid gently into bed and lay beside her. She stirred slightly, he held his breath for what seemed ages, frozen in his movements until he was satisfied she was still asleep

He lay awake looking up at the ceiling in the half-light. He could feel the warmth of her body against him. He thought of Jackie and the way she held him close. Inwardly he cried. He had committed a soul-destroying act which was to slowly invade his sanity – he felt sick. Sleep must have crept up on him eventually. It was well into the night when he felt her move and stretch a little. She yawned and turned towards him. 'Good morning darling!' She drew herself closer to him. He could feel her breasts bury themselves into his flesh.

'Do you want me?' she asked.

'No. Not today.' His own answer sickened him. He felt his guilt surge through his body.

'I understand darling, you have had a lot to think about.' She kissed him on the cheek. 'I'm here now darling to help – don't shut me out.'

She put her arms around him and drew herself nearer to him. They stayed like that for some time. He eventually said, 'Fancy a cup of tea?'

Gemma was busy attending to the children's breakfast the next morning, neither she or Robert felt like eating, their feelings running much too high.

More floral tributes arrived, together with cards of sympathy. Gemma looked hard at her children and wondered what was going on in their minds. This was the first time they had to say goodbye to someone they knew and loved. Poor kids – she thought.

Robert was returning from his walk with Sheba, who no doubt found the different landscape and sea smells intoxicating. Within a few yards of reaching his front gate, Ian White appeared to offer his condolences. Known to the locals as Snowy, he was probably the oldest on the island now that Alf Everitt had died. He was a second generation sheep farmer, taking over from his father some twenty years ago, and now at the age of 75 he had handed it over to his two sons.

Snowy knew Robert's father well when he was alive, and was now recalling some of the comical episodes they had shared. He was a stocky red-faced man with rimless spectacles, and a polished pate, save for a few strands of hair around his ears. Robert always thought he resembled a character from a Dickens novel. Eventually he said, 'See you later', no doubt referring to the funeral, and was off.

The tide was receding and with it came the hordes of gulls searching for molluscs and small crustaceans in the wet mud left behind by the tide. At 12.30 an uncanny strangeness hung like a heavy fog upon the air, even the receding waves retreated quietly, silence enveloped the island as it did for Bert, Sally and Alf. Then the sun made an appearance.

Cars were arriving from the mainland bringing friends, acquaintances and Robert's old aunt whom he had lived with during his school terms.

Gemma was getting ready upstairs. One or two close connections of Mary came to the cottage with their tributes, others went straight to the abbey. Nerves and anxiety was beginning to take over as Robert repeatedly looked at his watch or for any signs of the hearse. The village was standing still.

Five minutes later Gemma appeared from upstairs dressed entirely in black, looking both elegant and beautiful. A pang of guilt ran through him Walking towards her, he held out his arms, which was readily accepted. He held her against himself and hugged her as a tear ran down his face. 'You look lovely,' he whispered.

The great clock standing in the corner of the room ticked the time away. Robert was restless, pacing up and down the room, looking out of the window, until eventually he walked down the garden path and stood looking at the remains of his father's boat. He was conscious of the pain life can throw at you. He was aware that in happiness you can feel pain. He knew how cruel and ruthless life can be – it happened when he lost Linda, and now he was at its mercy again.

Gemma walked down the garden path to join him. 'Are you all right?'

'Yes, I'm OK.' She held his hand and squeezed it gently.

The sound of a car door being slammed made their heads turn to look along the garden path towards the road. It was Jackie with her daughter Roslin.

Jackie, dressed in black from head to foot, walked like a fashion model along the garden path to meet them. 'Hello Gemma,' she said, embracing her tightly. 'It is good to see you after all this time – but not under these circumstances.' Turning towards Robert she held out her arms to him. He stepped forward for her embrace. 'I'm sorry about Mary, it was quite a shock.' She kissed him on the cheek. 'I know you will miss her, we all will, she was such a dear.'

Gemma was talking to Roslin. 'Robert,' started Jackie, 'the last time I was here your mother did the catering for your dad's funeral. It all seems so unreal.'

He began to feel uncomfortable, not knowing what she was going to say next. The situation was saved by Gemma calling, 'They are here.'

* * *

80

The hearse drew up outside the cottage, two assistants gathering the floral tributes. The undertaker went inside the cottage with Robert's party. Sheba gave a soft bark as they entered. When the last wreath and floral tributes were in place, the main party took their place behind the hearse and followed on foot. The windows of the cottages en route had the curtains drawn as a mark of respect, their occupants waiting until the cortege had passed, then following. A bell tolled. The expected congregation was large, soft organ music greeted them as they entered. The sound of people coughing and shuffling of feet echoed around the walls, then silence.

The priest entered the pulpit and announced the first hymn.

The service over, the last notes of the hymn fading away, then the clanking of the latch on the door of the chapel sounded as the oak door opened, letting in a blast of cold air. The congregation stood as the coffin bearing Mary's body passed slowly by them, out into the late afternoon sun to the opened grave of her husband.

The vicar said a few words as the coffin was lowered, Jackie found Robert's hand and squeezed it as the Lord's Prayer was said – silence took over as they looked into the grave. His body seemed to move in jerks, his mouth went dry, he tried to speak. He wanted to say how dignified and lovely she looked. The vicar saved the situation by saying to Robert, 'At last they are together again – God be with them both.'

'Thank you,' was Robert's reply. Gemma moved towards him and touched his arm.

On the way back to the reception hall Robert put his hand on Graham's shoulder. 'Are you all right son?'

Graham just nodded his head, obviously overcome by the whole event.

In the reception hall Jack Mason went over to Robert. 'Well Doc, it is all over now. It is a great shame, the whole island will miss her, as they did Bert. So what happens now? Are you going to sell or keep the cottage?'

'Keeping it, Jack. I'm going to use it to escape from the mad world out there.'

'Good for you, it's yours now, you were born here, I am pleased. Sorry about your mother, it is a pity it turned out the way it did.'

'Thank you again Jack, now you take care of yourself.'

Gemma was in the kitchen waiting for the kettle to boil when Robert and Graham walked in. Jackie was sitting on the settee with Zoe and Roslin looking through a magazine together. 'Hello Robert, feeling better now?' Jackie said as he entered.

'I suppose so, it has been quite a week. I feel now I just want to get lost for a few weeks and relax, somewhere far away.'

'I know the feeling.' She looked at him with a look he was getting to know very well. 'Somewhere warm and not too many people.'

'Yes Utopia, do you know where it is?'

Gemma reappeared with a tray and placed it on the table.

'I don't know if you feel the same,' she started, 'but there seems to be an emptiness now, not just in this cottage, but outside, it seemed to follow wherever I went.'

She placed the cups on the table as Jackie shot a glance towards Robert.

'Can't say I felt it, Gemma. Not a feeling of being watched, if that is what you mean, but I sometimes get a feeling of loneliness, despair and abandonment, wondering what am I doing here.'

'I am sorry Jackie, I didn't think,' Gemma said quickly. 'It must be difficult for you bringing up Roslin on your own. I know you cannot do it at the moment but will you eventually go out to Switzerland to live when Roslin has finished college?'

Robert felt uneasy the way the conversation was going.

'Frankly Gemma I just don't know at the moment, there are so many factors to consider.' Zoe drew her attention to a picture in the magazine. 'Well Jackie you can always come and visit us for a few days.'

'Thank you Gemma. I might just take you up on that.'

The sound of cars going past the window made Jackie look at the big clock. 'Well folks, I must be getting back. Now keep in touch and take care.' She kissed Zoe, saying, 'Perhaps one day I'll see her ride.' Gemma and Robert escorted her and Roslin to the car outside, Jackie put her arms around Gemma's neck saying, 'Look after Robert and the children. See you all soon.'

'Drive carefully,' said Gemma as she opened the car door.

The car came alive and with a quick wave of her hand she drove off.

Gemma returned to the cottage leaving Robert outside standing in the road. He stood there watching the car diminish in size as it sped away from him, taking with it a part of his life. He felt choked as his eyes moistened. Memories of the last few days and thoughts raced through his mind. Guilt was pushed aside. The present occasion which brought her to him today once more loomed before him tearing him apart. The gross dishonesty and betrayal of his wife and family, and the uncertainty of ever seeing Jackie again was only the beginning of the torture which was to follow. The vibrant flame of passion within him would burn for a long time yet.

'Farcroft' once consisted of three old barns but the developers had done a really first class job on converting it into a most modern and desirable residence in the heart of Charnwood Forest, a much sort-after area near the two reservoirs Swithland and Cropston. Under a cloudless sky, Gemma set off with Sheba for a walk through Bradgate Park, once the home of Lady Jane Grey, the nine-days queen of England. Entering through the large wooden gates, Sheba now off the lead and running in circles on front of her, Gemma approached the ruined remains of Lady Jane's house to her right. Outside it two peacocks paraded on the lawn, proudly displaying their colourful tails and keeping a watchful eye on Sheba until she was safely past. The sound of rippling water passing beneath a low bridge and a dog emerging from the stream shaking itself in a flurry of spray, having retrieved a stick thrown in by its master, made Gemma smile to herself. She walked into the avenue of very old oak trees bordering either side of the path to the outcrop of huge granite rocks which protruded through sparse grass and brown bracken, towards the Victorian Folly known as Old John. It had been built in memory of a gardener who once worked on the estate and lost his life while attending to a bonfire.

It was five years since the death of Mary Watts. They had visited Lindisfarne on several occasions since, but Robert had not really got over the loss. Gemma had constantly reminded him there were other places to go for a holiday but he always won her over by saying Graham loved his fishing and Zoe loved her riding at the farm.

The shrieks of children and the sound of traffic from the main road leading into Newtown Linford made her realise she had walked the full length of the park and it was necessary to turn back.

Back home Gemma took off her walking shoes and settled back in the armchair, tired but refreshed after her long walk in the park, and fell asleep. Zoe was the first home and made a pot of tea, taking a cup in to Gemma who was still asleep in the chair. Zoe tapped her gently on the shoulder, saying, 'Come on, rise and shine!'

Robert arrived later with a surprise for Gemma. He had been working at the Leicester Art Gallery and Museum and had managed to obtain two tickets for a symphony concert at the De Montfort Hall in Leicester. Music had always played an important part in her life before her marriage, but now musical evenings were a very rare event in Gemma's life, so tonight was something special.

As she listened intently to the London Philharmonic Orchestra playing Rachmaninov's Piano Concerto, tears filled her eyes as the last chords were played. She found Robert's hand and squeezed it gently.

Out in the cool night air, the strains of the music still ringing in her ears, she smiled weakly at him as she clung to his arm. 'Thank you darling that was beautiful.'

The lights of 'Farcroft' came into view as they turned off the main Leicester/Loughborough road. Graham was already preparing supper as they walked in. 'Enjoy the show?' he asked.

'Lovely thanks, very enjoyable,' replied Gemma.

'Oh Jackie rang earlier, asked what time you would be back, I said I wasn't sure but should be back by ten-thirty.'

'Shall I ring her now?'

'Let us have a drink first, it can't be that important,' said Robert, taking off his shoes.

Gemma went into the hall and picked up the phone and rang Jackie.

'Hi Gemma,' came a voice from the other end of the line. 'Did you enjoy the concert? Graham told me were you had gone.'

'Yes thank you. Is anything wrong?'

'I was reading our local newspaper earlier today . . . I'll read it out to you.

'"A young woman was found dead in a car park in Coldstream on Tuesday. Early morning workers noticed a woman in a car with her head thrown back as if asleep. When they failed to rouse her they contacted the police. She was taken to hospital where it was discovered that she had died of a heart attack sometime in the previous afternoon. She was described as being in her late forties, very well dressed and attractive. In the boot of her car were a number of cardboard boxes containing ladies underwear. Identification papers found in her handbag name her as Francis Broadbent."'

'On no,' gasped Gemma. 'Poor Fran.'

'An inquest will be held next week.'

'What an end . . . alone in a car park. She was always so lively a prefect at school, hockey captain, married, divorced . . . The last time I met her was at your place when I first met Robert. What a tragedy Jackie . . . I am sorry'.

'I'll let you know what happens. I may go to her funeral when I know when it is.'

'How about you? Are you all right?'

'Oh fine, Roslin passed her driving test some time ago, has her own car now. Several boy friends, nothing serious. Remember Kathy Stubbs as was? Her husband was killed on New Year's Eve some time ago now. I hear she is seeing some-one again whose wife died two years ago. I just hope it turns out all right for her, she needs some luck.'

'What about you, apart from your concert, any news?'

'Zoe is doing well with her horse riding, Graham has passed his driving test and is seeing a very nice girl from Quorn. He is still in the engineering.'

'What about Robert, is he well?'

'Oh yes Jackie. Still lecturing and going abroad quite a lot, you know, the usual stuff.'

'I was just wondering Gemma, if Fran is still named as Frances Broadbent it looks as if she never re-married, so who will make her final arrangements unless her own parents are still alive?'

'Don't know Jackie. Who would have thought that she would end up in a car park – alone'.

'It really doesn't bear thinking about. None of us know how we shall end up – but I want to end my days in my own bed.'

Gemma laughed.

ELEVEN

Early in the Spring of 2003 Gemma stood in the doorway of the conservatory dressed in a thick pullover, anorak and wellington boots holding a basket full of weeds recently pulled from the flowerbeds. She stood admiring her work and the sea of daffodils surrounding the large lawn. She stood motionless with a suggestion of a smile on her face, not from her accomplishment in the garden, but at the sound of a thrush in full song high in one of the trees stripped of its foliage. A few wisps of cirrus cloud in a pale blue sky and a weak sun heralded a lovely day, with a slight chill in the air making exhaled breath visible like a mist, and the reddening of the nose and lobes of her ears. Somewhere in the distance a tractor was busy preparing the soil for the next set of crops. Like the background of a symphony of springtime sounds she stood there as if rooted, recalling her musical interests, 'On hearing the first cuckoo in Spring'.

The sound of the telephone ringing in the hallway brought her back to the land of reality.

Taking off her boots she entered the hall and picked up the receiver.

'Hello Gemma, it's your mum. You know your Dad has for some time now had difficulty in a certain area, I kept telling him to go to the doctor but you know how stubborn he can be. Anyway he finally went, and now he's in hospital in Preston. Gemma, your dad has prostate cancer. I went to see him yesterday and he is very poorly. One of the doctors said he should have had treatment long before now. They are giving him treatment now, I don't know if it is chemotherapy but he looks awful. Gemma, he has been in so much pain he looks like an old man. He has been wearing a catheter for weeks. I'm sorry to have to tell you this, I'm going to ring your sister now but I'm not too sure of the time difference. When they had finished the tests they told him he had prostate hyperplasia, whatever that is, but he looks really ill.'

'Do you want me to come over to you?'

86

'I don't know what to tell you to do . . .'

'Wait until Robert comes home and I will discuss it with him.'

Replacing the receiver, she walked slowly back again to the conservatory doorway. How horribly different it all seemed now. The song thrush had finished singing, the tractor noise had ceased and a strange quietness hung about the countryside where moments ago there had been magic. As the cool air wrapped itself around her, the thought of her father in hospital and the sense of panic in her mother's voice, left her uneasy and frustrated.

The rest of the day dragged slowly on. Soon the family would be home and the situation discussed, but Gemma knew inwardly she must go to Preston Hospital.

Gemma arrived at the hospital the following afternoon, introducing herself to the senior nurse, explaining that she had travelled quite a distance to see her father.

The nurse brought her up to date about his condition as they walked along towards the ward.

At first sight she caught her breath, seeing her father lying on his back, pale faced and drawn. His cheeks were sunken, eyes closed and mouth wide open. A plastic tube had been inserted into his nose, held in position with tape, and another tube fitted into his forearm and led to a bottle suspended on a portable stand beside the bed. On the bedside cabinet was a display of flowers, three get well cards, a small clock, a jug of water and a box of men's tissues. The nurse turned towards her, indicating with her hand to go closer to his bed, saying, 'I'll leave you with him,' and quietly walked away.

Gemma looked at her father as if rooted to the spot. This motionless slowly breathing figure lying still, devoid of all colour, was once full of life and vitality with a healthy complexion. She moved over to him. He never stirred. Touching his arm gently and stroking it she whispered, 'Dad, it's me, Gemma, I have come to see you.' She paused. 'Mum told me you were in here, that's why I have come.' There was a slight movement on his face. His eyes opened slightly as his head turned towards her. He made a slight sign of recognition with a weak smile.

'Mum is coming later. I came straight here from home,' still stroking his arm. 'You gave us quite a shock when we knew what happened.'

He began to cough as he attempted to reach his tissues. The very act of coughing seemed to exhaust him. He lay back on his pillow breathing deeply, his arms falling by his side. He remained like that for several minutes, looking up at the ceiling, and all Gemma could do was feel her eyes filling as her vision became blurred.

She was still sitting there when a familiar figure approached the bed. Her mother, Doreen. Gemma sprang from her chair and embraced her, holding back the tears.

'Have you been here long?' asked her mother.

'Nearly two hours. I've been trying to talk to him but he seems so far away all the time.'

'I know dear he is with me – look, if you want a break, a coffee or something, I'm here now, so off you go.'

'Yes I think I will.' Touching her father's arm again she walked off down the ward, turning her head to look back as she passed through the door.

Holding back her tears she made her way to the canteen and ordered a pot of tea and a teacake. She sat looking out onto the garden and the gardener attending the flowerbeds, daffodils rocking slightly in the breeze between the border of primroses.

Sipping her tea slowly a puzzled look came over her face. She put the teacup down, deep in thought, reasoning that if her father had survived the operation for prostate cancer, surely he should be making good progress now, on the way to full recovery. She took another sip of tea. Something was not quite right. With this uppermost in her mind she was determined to see the sister in charge and get the truth.

She did not have far to go. Having finished her tea she walked out into the corridor and saw the sister coming towards her.

'Oh hello,' she began, 'as you know when I first came, I am the daughter of Mr Barclay who has had an operation for prostate cancer. Could you please tell me exactly what the situation is, as I think he looks extremely ill though he should be on the way by now for complete recovery.'

'I'm sorry Mrs . . .'

'Watts, Gemma Watts.'

'Come with me, I will get Dr Culman to see you.'

Gemma followed behind her into the office. Seated at a desk under the window of his office was Dr Culman, a middle aged man of foreign appearance. He looked up from behind a pile of folders in front of him as they entered. Putting his pen down he leaned back in his chair looked at them over his thick black-framed glasses, then leaned forward, resting his hands on the desk in front of him. Gemma noticed he wore a gold ring with a large ruby on it, gold cufflinks and a very large wristwatch.

'This is Mrs Watts, the daughter of Mr Barclay in my ward who recently underwent an operation for prostate. She's somewhat concerned about his slow progress.'

'Ah, yes, Barclay . . .' He leaned back in his chair, looking at Gemma. 'Just a moment while I get his file out.' He rose from his chair and beckoning them both to take a seat. The sister interrupted by saying, 'If you will excuse me, I am needed on the ward with the doctor.'

'Yes, of course, Sister.'

Gemma took a seat and looked about the room as the consultant searched through a pile of folders. A framed print of 'A Woman Crying' by Picasso took her eye. She was still looking at it when, 'Ah, here we are, Barclay . . .' Sitting down again he turned over the pages of papers in the folder, having briefly scanned a few sheets. Eventually he said in a low voice, 'According to the notes I have before me, your father had an operation for prostate hyperplasia, which is common in men over the age of say – fifty.' He looked at her over his glasses, then continued, 'In itself that is a straightforward operation today, but your father had other complications in a different area over a longer period of time which he never sought advice about or reported. When he did realise he was in serious trouble he set alarm bells ringing. As I have just said, the operation for prostate was easy and normally he would have been making a complete recovery by now, but the second problem was not so straightforward. Your father must have suffered a great deal of discomfort and distress over a long period of time. He had pancreatic cancer, which affects as many as 7,000 people alone in the UK. It is most difficult to treat because, as in your father's case, by the time its victims do realise they need help it is well advanced and they are in real trouble. It nearly always, I repeat nearly always, proves fatal. It is very resistant to traditional chemotherapy and radiation.'

Gemma sat motionless, hanging on to his every word. He continued:

'Mrs Watts, I am sorry to have to tell you this, but they are the facts – that is why you see him in the condition he is in today. Had he alerted us earlier we might have had a chance, but it was only discovered when he came in for a straightforward operation. With the grace of God we MIGHT get him through this, but prepare yourself for the worst. It is going to be hard for you and your mother to come to terms with.' He closed the file and sat looking at her as her eyes filled up.

'I'm sorry to have to tell you this, no-one likes to hear news like that and I just wish it could have been better. Did he not say anything about how he felt?'

'I don't live at home now, I live in Leicestershire.'

'What about your mother, did she suspect anything?'

'No – the first I heard that anything was wrong was last night on the phone.'

They both sat in silence for what seemed an eternity, then Gemma said, 'Thank you, doctor,' taking a tissue from her handbag and applying it to her eyes.

'Rest assured we will do everything we can.'

Gemma composed herself as she walked back to the ward. Her mother was still holding her father's hand and talking to him as he lay back on the pillow. Drawing up a chair beside her mother, 'Any response?' she asked.

'No, did you get something to eat?'

'Yes thanks,' Gemma replied, careful not to divulge anything at this stage. They both sat at the side of the bed watching him drifting in and out of drowsiness. Gemma's mother was continually talking to him as the afternoon moved on, and Gemma was finding it hard not to blurt out the truth.

The silence in the ward, save for the occasional coughing of one of the patients, was broken by movement at the entrance. The tea trolley had arrived.

'I think we should be going now Mum.'

'Why?'

'The nurses will be wanting to change him and attend to his dressings, and the drug trolley will be along soon, you know all that kind of thing, besides we cannot do anything for him now we will only be in the way.'

Gemma stood up and replaced her chair against the wall.

'Yes I suppose you are right,' her mother replied, bending over the bed to kiss her husband on the cheek.

The cool afternoon air met them as they crossed the hospital car park. There was a distinct silence between them as Gemma opened her car door for her mother.

Doreen was the first to break the silence. 'It is much easier by car Gemma, I waited ages for a bus coming.'

'Did you?' answered Gemma.

'Well, what did you think of your Dad?'

Gemma gulped as she pulled up at traffic lights, 'He is very poorly, Mum.'

'Yes he is. I think we should go away somewhere warm when he comes home. What do you think?'

Gemma remained silent, giving her a quick glance, fighting desperately not to tell her the truth just yet. The time was not right.

The rest of the journey was small talk until eventually they pulled up outside a well maintained semi-detached house in Chorley. Her parents had lived there for many years, moving in when Gemma was twelve. It was from this house that Gemma's older sister Maria married before setting off for South Africa to live. Gemma married Robert three years later, working in Edinburgh but married from this address. Once inside the house Gemma kicked off her shoes and sank into an easy chair.

'I'll put the kettle on – We will have a meal later.'

'That is fine, Mum.'

'I must get some fruit for tomorrow for him, grapes and things,' she said, disappearing into the kitchen.

Gemma lay back in the chair and closed her eyes, wondering when the right moment would arrive to tell her the truth.

Ten minutes passed, and Gemma's mother appeared carrying a tray. 'Mum, have you told Maria?'

'Your sister? Of course I have.' She put the tray down on a small table.

'What did she say?'

'They were both very sorry to hear he was in hospital and hoped he would be home very soon.'

'Mum – Did Dad ever tell you how he felt these last few weeks?'

'You know your Dad, he never mentioned anything like that. He never spoke of things like that, in fact he wouldn't tell you if he was dying.'

That last remark stopped Gemma in her tracks. She took a deep breath and started again. 'When I went out to the canteen to get something to eat when you came in today, I started thinking about how ill he looked. I thought after two or three days following an operation of that nature he should be sitting up now and talking, you know, feeling better, taking notice.'

'It is early days yet, Gemma.'

'No Mum, it is NOT early days. Dad is very ill. I went to see the consultant Dr Culman in his office. He told me the operation for prostate was a straightforward one, but what you did NOT know, and what THEY did not know until later when they operated was he has pancreatic cancer in a very advanced stage, a disease which can be fatal if left too late – and Dad never reported it to his doctor.'

'Oh God Gemma, he never said anything to me – poor Andrew!'

'Did he not give you any idea he was in trouble?'

'No. He just took a little longer in the bathroom. I had no idea he was dealing with a problem.'

'Mum, you have got to face the facts, he may not be coming home.'

'Oh NO Gemma, don't say that!' She started to sob. 'Why did he not tell me he was in trouble, I would have made him go to the doctor . . .'

'Perhaps he knew and was afraid of the truth, he must have known it was serious and did not want you to worry.'

Just after 2.00 pm the following day, they both arrived at the hospital. Gemma's Mum almost ran along the corridor to the ward. As Gemma entered the ward her heart almost stopped. Her father's bed had been moved and was now next to the nurse's desk. She knew instantly the significance of this move and felt sick in the stomach.

Her mother hurried to her husband's bedside and kissed him on the cheek. He was sitting almost upright. Gemma stood back and observed from the end of the bed. His face looked waxen, pale and yellowish, tubes and wires were attached to various parts of his body, a plastic breathing mask covered the lower part of his face. His eyes remained closed and he breathed slowly.

She drew closer to his bed, 'Hello Dad, it's Gemma.'

There was a slight response, his eyes opened to a slit, she moved over and kissed him on the forehead then drew back looking at this person lying lifeless, breathing slowly, his arms outside the covers, sunken cheeks and lips dry and cracked.

Both sat talking to him, though no response ever came, not even the slightest sign of acknowledgment. Gemma looked about the ward. The occupants were mainly elderly. Some lay on top of their beds reading, others dosed off. One old gentleman waved to her and smiled. She responded.

Time dragged, each time she looked at the clock over the entrance door it seemed to have moved very little. Conversation had now finished, there was little point in trying. Doreen sat holding her husband's hand stroking it from time to time.

A nurse entered the ward and walked towards them. Taking a chart from the bottom of the bed she stood reading it, then said, 'I just want to take his temperature,' and brushing past Gemma she adjusted the bottles and watched the flow. 'Feeling a bit drowsy are we today?' she said. Having checked the flow of liquid in the bottle attached to his arm, she made a note of it and replaced it. 'Not talking today, Mr Barclay? It is a bit cold outside but you are nice and warm. I'll just tidy you up a bit.' She rearranged the pillows and cards on the bedside cabinet, took his temperature then entered the reading on the chart. 'Don't go to sleep, soon be time for your tablets.'

She returned to the desk and joined two other nurses just yards away. An orderly appeared accompanied by a nurse pushing a bed into a vacant space in the ward. Its occupant, covered by a blanket, looked elderly judging by the grey hair just visible above the covering. The curtain was then pulled around the bed, thus ending the floor show. Other visitors entered the ward, some carrying flowers, others fruit or magazines. Gemma looked towards her father lying pale and motionless as if asleep, in contrast to the ward becoming alive with conversation and a few quiet laughs. Fear and doubt overtook Gemma as she began to realise the end was drawing near. Looking at her mother bending over this lifeless form, stroking his arm gently, brought a lump to her throat. He WAS dying, but her mother would not accept the fact. When it did come adjustments would have to be made to her life. Living without your life's partner would be difficult, but she knew her mother would cope. She was sure of that.

Gemma excused herself on the pretext that she was going to the toilet, but stopped as the nurse was leaving the desk. The information she received was as expected, this she would relate to her mother later.

It was getting dark outside when they both emerged from the warmth of the hospital and met the cool air. It had rained during the afternoon leaving pools of water in the car park. Gemma and her mother sat in silence on the way home, each trying to avoid the obvious. Car headlights of oncoming traffic dazzled on the wet surface of the road as they passed throwing up sprays of water, so that with the car's windscreen wipers needed to be on fast.

Once inside the house Gemma searched desperately for the right moment to tell her mother the situation her father was in as told by the nurse, so she could be prepared. That moment was elusive. The chance never seemed right, her mother was putting on a brave face, sometimes humming to herself in the kitchen as she prepared the meal.

'I think Southport would be fine for your father to recuperate, it's not too far to travel and there is plenty of sand to sit in a deck-chair and relax, it would do him good.'

'Mother, 'Gemma began, ' I don't think you should build your hopes up too high yet, the condition is critical. He may not be coming back.'

'I know Gemma, I know, I just hope . . .' throwing her arms around Gemma's neck and hugging her tightly.

The following day was wet. Their visit to the bedside watching their loved one breathing slowly and not responding to any conversation was an ordeal in itself. Gemma knew inwardly this could be the last time she would see him. Memories of earlier times flashed across her mind, when this lifeless body now lying before her was full of fun and laughter. Remembering how he would take her in the car for her music lessons and how he admired her playing. The holidays by the sea. The pride he showed when she gained her BSc degree in chemistry and the day he walked her down the aisle for her marriage to Robert. So much had taken place between them and now the light of life was dimming, his life was almost over and she would be left with memories and photographs, but this scene before her now would remain with her for some time to come.

The following morning Gemma after a restless night was up early making a cup of tea with the lights in the kitchen on at 6.30 am. The day outside was dark and cold.

Climbing the stairs with a cup of tea for her mother, as she reached a point halfway up the telephone rang, shattering the silence in the house. She froze. It was the call she did not want to hear. The voice on the other end of the line informed her that her father had slipped away peacefully during the night.

The afternoon was still cold but the forecast did not mention rain. The past two weeks had been hectic and the strain was beginning to tell on Gemma, but now the day of the funeral had arrived. Gemma's sister Maria had arrived from South Africa, Robert and Zoe arrived earlier leaving Graham behind. Various aunts and uncles dressed in black moved about the room uneasily making polite conversation. Robert's own thoughts surfaced of his own parents and the tragic circumstances surrounding them. The room went silent as a voice said, 'They are here.' Suddenly as if switched on by an unseen hand everyone began to move and adjust their clothing, checking their appearance in the mirror on the wall and turned facing the door, waiting.

The small stone church in Chorley brought back memories to Gemma as the low sounds of the organ being played reminded her of the day she took her father's arm and walked down the aisle to become Mrs Watts, so many years ago. She looked at her mother and gave a weak smile, then took her arm. Her sister Maria sat next to her, crying openly.

The service was short but emotional, referring to the time her father spent in the RAF during the war in North Africa. After the war he worked in Customs and Excise in Edinburgh, a position he held until his retirement. Afterwards he moved to Chorley in Lancashire to be near his widowed mother who unfortunately died four years after they moved in. The sight of the Pennines, the nearness of the sea and easy access to the Lake District was an added bonus.

The last few moments round the open grave were proving too much for Doreen, taking all Gemma and Maria's strength to prevent her jumping into the grave.

TWELVE

Gemma sat at the writing desk in 'Farcroft' answering a letter from her sister in South Africa. She was reassuring her that her mother was coping living on her own. Although the conditions on which they had met were not ideal, it was good to see her again. Nearly three months had passed since the funeral, the day temperature had risen, the skies were less cloudy and the garden was coming back to life again with butterflies, bees, flowers and blossom on the trees and bushes.

Robert was away in Sedgeford, a small village in Norfolk, for a week where an ongoing dig was in operation of an early settlers' site. Zoe was preparing for her final examination for the City and Guilds Hairdressing Certificate and Graham was away in France with his girlfriend. Life for Gemma was much quieter now after the last few weeks.

Zoe looked up from her papers spread out on the table in front of her. 'Oh Mum, I might be staying at Pip's on Saturday if that is OK? Her Dad is away at the weekend, her mother says I can stay if I want.'

'Yes dear that is OK.'

Pip and Zoe had become great friends, both sharing the same horse stables at Quorn, meeting up with other riders from the same stables.

'Looks as if I am going to be on my own then this week-end. Your father away, Graham away, and now you. Ah well, I can't fall out with anyone can I?' she laughed.

'Yes, it is times like this you miss a dog.' Zoe picked up her papers spread out on the table 'Yes, poor Sheba, she was a good dog,' replied Gemma.

The telephone rang in the hall. Gemma left her desk to answer it. Gemma picked up the telephone receiver.

'Hi Helen, how good to hear you! How are you? Oh . . . That will better for you . . . I'm so pleased for you . . . Is he? . . . That is one good thing . . . I know you did not like it much . . .

And he is making good progress . . . that is fine . . . When he is mobile again you must bring him over to us . . . would love to see you and the baby of course ... How is she? ... Good ... And you are keeping all right yourself? ... Yes you have ... All right Helen ... We are all fine this end now that everything has settled down again, but what a time it was ... Let us hope so ... Thank you for telling me ... I will ... You take care ... Me too ... Bye Helen ... Bye.'

Returning to the room again, 'That was Helen,' she said to Zoe. 'They are living in Edinburgh again near to where we lived before we both got married. Her husband is still off work after being knocked off his moped in Brussels, but it will be better for them now. I'd like to see them both again. I expect Monica has changed, anyway. Clear your stuff from the table and we will get some lunch.'

'I've finished all I'm going to do today ... I want to go round to the stables this afternoon and see Ridge.'

'Getting nervous?'

'ME, no, not a bit.'

The scent of honeysuckle creeping along the trellis, bunches of wisteria hanging like lanterns, and rhododendrons surrounding the lawn on a very hot cloudless afternoon in June found Gemma on a sun lounger wearing a bikini top and shorts, a glass of cool lemonade and a novel by her side. Robert had returned from Norfolk two days ago and was busy writing his notes indoors. Zoe had gone to exercise Ridge in readiness for the forthcoming horse trials at the weekend. Graham was rarely at home, either working or with his girlfriend in nearby Loughborough. After the turmoil of the last few months this was bliss to Gemma. As the afternoon moved on so did the temperature, reaching into the eighties.

Robert emerged from the house wearing only shorts and sandals. 'Don't overdo it in this hot sun Gemma, there is a lot of heat in it today.'

He stood beside her. 'I've been thinking,' he began, 'how about spending a few days in the cottage by the sea. It's been ages since we were last there.'

'It would certainly make a change ... See what Zoe thinks after the trials.'

'No use having a place by the sea and not using it.'

'It won't be like it used to be. It's been locked up for ages.' She took a sip from her glass of lemonade.

'All the more reason for going, make sure everything is all right. Besides all that lovely clean fresh air going to waste!'

* * *

Saturday morning came, Zoe was first up and dressed in her riding habit. The sky was cloudless, not a breath of wind and even at this early hour it had all the signs of being very hot. A perfect day for spectators at the horse trials, but not for the horses.

' 'Morning love,' Gemma came into the kitchen. 'Had your breakfast?'

'I don't feel like eating yet Mum, I'll get something when I get there.'

'You are sure?'

'Yes Pip's father will be here soon to pick me up. I'll be all right, just a bit uptight. I have to settle down before Ridge sees me. He is very sensitive and I want him at his best today.'

'Is Pip riding Forester?' Gemma asked.

'Yes, Mr Sedley says we make a good team. I expect he is there now with the horses giving them plenty of time to settle down.'

'Just be careful dear and good luck. We will be along later.'

Zoe, clearly on edge, walked up and down the kitchen looking at the clock on the wall every two minutes.

'Why don't you walk down the garden? It might settle you.'

'I just wish they would hurry up, I hate this hanging about.'

Twenty minutes passed. Zoe's patience clearly at its limit, Gemma remained silent lest she lit a fuse.

Like a fanfare of trumpets heralding the arrival of some important dignitary, the sound of a car horn outside broke the tension. Zoe sprang into action, and picking up her hold-all and kissing Gemma on the cheek she was out of the door and running across the gravel path to the waiting car in record time.

Shrieks of laughter came from the car when Zoe got into the back with Pip. Gemma followed, making her way to the car to thank Pip's father for taking her.

Pip's father was a red faced man of portly proportions with a permanent cheery smile on his face.

'Good morning – what a lovely day,' said Gemma. 'I hope everything goes off all right and you both win trophies. Thank you for taking Zoe.'

'It is no trouble Mrs Watts. Hope to see you there – Bye.' Gemma stood watching the car drive away.

Returning to the house, she paused before entering, watching butterflies dancing between the flower beds. She smiled to herself. A group of walkers on the way to Bradgate Park passed, laughing as they went, they could not be seen and the sound of their footsteps seemed unmistakably softer than in winter, as though the gathered dust were smothering their fall.

Robert had promised he would be back in time to get to the horse trials. Much to the annoyance of Gemma he had accepted an invitation at short notice to attend a seminar at Leicester University of mixed students studying Geology, Architecture and Astronomy, recommended by Professor Herbert Heyman, a great friend of Robert's over many years. He was no stranger to this university. Over the years he had given illustrated lectures in his own subject during which time their friendship developed. They had discussed writing a book together dealing with astro-physics, the creation of the universe and early life on the planet.

Gemma was in the kitchen preparing sandwiches and drinks for their day at the horse trials at Burghley House in Lincolnshire, one of the biggest Elizabethan mansions in the country. The horse trials there are an annual event. Gemma was gradually getting more and more annoyed with Robert as time moved on. But any trace of anger soon disappeared when she heard a car draw up outside.

The hot sun beat down on the car as Robert made his way across country through Melton Mowbray towards Oakham heading for the A1 and Stamford. The undulating road stretched before them as the road turned sharply on the brow of a hill where a small column of cars stood waiting for a set of temporary road traffic lights which seemed permanently fixed on red. A large JCB digger was working surrounded by four men in yellow jackets, cordoned off by red and white cones occupying half the width of the road.

After what seemed a lifetime the traffic lights eventually turned to green and the long procession of cars moved forward, passing the workmen and two lorries parked within the cordoned off area. Having passed the last cone the cars in front gradually increased their speed. Almost immediately Robert's car lurched to one side and limped along.

'What the ...' he said bringing the car to a halt. On inspection the front nearside tyre was flat. 'Now what?' asked Gemma, getting out of the car to look.

'What do you mean – now what?' was the irritated reply. 'Change the bloody tyre, that's what.'

Gemma stood by the side of the road as she watched Robert remove objects from the car boot then lift the spare wheel out.

'It would happen to-day when we are short of time,' he muttered between breaths. 'We'll probably miss Zoe's ride now.'

Gemma's heart sank at that last remark. 'And whose fault is that?' she snapped.

'What do you mean by that?' He retorted

'You and your damned seminar, today of all days! Why did you have to go? All those weeks of preparation for today when we should be there to support her, ruined because you could not say NO for once; the most important event of her year put in jeopardy! We might as well go straight back home when you have fixed it – it's is almost 3 o'clock now.'

It was well after 3.0 pm when they arrived at the Show Ground in stony silence. Gemma had accused him of short-sightedness. He had defended himself by saying a puncture could happen to anyone, anytime.

After parking the car at the showground in the late afternoon they made their way to the arena, distancing themselves as much as possible from each other.

Approaching the official at the gate they were greeted with, 'Good afternoon.'

'Good afternoon,' replied Robert. 'We had a bit of trouble way back, blasted puncture. Have we missed much?'

A casualty earlier on, broken collarbone, horse slipped on the wet grass.'

'Wet grass?'

'Yes we had a short sharp shower early on about 11.00 am.'

A single male rider had just entered the arena as they took up their position in the enclosure. Bringing his horse to a standstill he raised his cap to the seated officials then took up his starting position. Some spectators moved to a better vantage point about the course.

Gemma turned to see a group of young people talking and laughing amongst themselves, some in rider attire.

'Hi Mum,' came a voice from the within the group.

Gemma turned swiftly in the direction of the voice. 'Hello darling,' she said. They embraced.

'Feeling relaxed now?'

'Yes Mum, I wish I had gone a little faster now but I did not want to risk losing any points, anyway I got a third. Not bad, eh!'

'Not bad darling, I think you did well.'

'Congratulations!' said Robert, joining them.

'Did you see how easily he jumps with his ears well back, he is lovely!'

'Er . . . no, Zoe,' Gemma said, looking towards Robert and raising her eyebrows.

'We were late getting here Zoe. We had a puncture. I'm sorry we missed you,' he said sheepishly.

'You mean you did not see any of it? That is bloody fine. The most important day in my life and you never saw any of it!'

'I'm sorry, it could not be helped, we had a puncture on the way, it could happen to anyone.'

'And it just happened today – well thank you very much – I hope you get another one on the way back home.' She stormed off leaving him looking crestfallen.

Gemma walked away slowly to join other spectators at the water-jump.

THIRTEEN

Six weeks had passed since the horse trials, the feud between Zoe and her father long forgotten. She now had her sights set on the City and Guilds Hairdressing exams. With only two more lectures to give before the summer recess Robert was already getting excited about the holiday in the cottage on Lindisfarne. Meanwhile Gemma had gone to her mother in Chorley who after eighteen months since the funeral of her husband was finding it difficult to manage on her own and had decided to move house.

During the first few days of her stay in Chorley, they had visited several house agents, looked at advertisements in local newspapers and traversed the streets and roads in the surrounding area looking for 'For Sale' notices. A feeling of despair was beginning to set in as they pursued their quest. Turning into a side road lined with tall plane trees just off the main road, they spotted a large Victorian house standing well back, at its entrance a very large notice board offering FLAT CONVER-SIONS FOR SALE. Gemma stopped the car. A wide gravelled path bordered with bushes and flowerbeds led to a very large imposing late Victorian redbrick house. Walking down the wide path past a small van with its rear doors opened wide, they approached the sound of hammering coming from the interior.

A man in a dark suit appeared in the doorway carrying a bunch of papers. Gemma approached him as he descended the four steps leading up to the massive oak front door.

'Good afternoon,' she began, 'we saw your noticeboard at the top of the drive about flats.'

'Ah yes – Are you interested?' He stopped at the foot of the steps.

'It's for my mother, she is thinking of moving.'

'The top flat was sold only two days ago.'

'We don't want a top flat, thank you.'

'Oh, we do have a lift . . .' was the quick reply. 'These flats are built to a very high standard, as you will see if you would like to look round.'

They followed him into a very spacious entrance hall. 'The whole place was gutted and rebuilt from scratch.'

Around the tiled floor of the hall several panelled doors led off. A wide imposing stairway took centre stage. Gemma saw the expression on her mother's face as they were taken from room to room. 'There are two bedrooms, a large lounge, and a beautifully fitted bathroom and kitchen, The flat comes with a fitted fridge, washing machine and dishwasher.' He turned and faced them. 'And that's it . . .' throwing his arms wide.

'And the price?' asked Gemma.

'We may be able to negotiate.'

'What do you think Mum?' asked Gemma as they walked slowly back to their car.

'I'm impressed,' was the reply. 'All new and beautifully finished, and no gardening.'

'You would be expected to contribute to that,' corrected Gemma.

They sat in the car looking at the house, surrounded by trees, neatly trimmed lawn and colourful flowerbeds, the winding path leading up to the attractive oak front door, and this impressive redbrick Victorian house with its blue diaper brickwork and tall ornamental chimneys and large double glazed bay windows was indeed an address to be proud of.

'It is off the main road so it should be reasonably quiet, and the bus stop is just round the corner – look just there,' Gemma pointed.

'Easy for getting into town . . .'

Gemma looked at her mother's face and saw a distinct change. She was transformed from a lonely widow to a completely new person with a renewed purpose in life. Gemma could not help but feel a tinge of regret if the sale went through. Not going back to her old address where she grew up, went to school from, was married from years ago – but some things have to change, and living in this new attractive area in a modernised flat would renew her mother's will to get on with life once again.

'You can have a flat on the second floor, it would be cheaper for you,' said Gemma.

'No I like the one we saw, a ground floor flat.'

The next few days were spent with the house agent's valuation of her house and getting it on the market, arranging for a deposit on the flat, looking at curtain material, carpets etc. together with all the necessary paperwork. By the end of the week most of the preparations had been done and it was time for Gemma to go back to her family.

* * *

103

Gemma arrived back at 'Farcroft' in the late afternoon to an empty, quiet house, giving her time to relax after her journey before the family arrived back. Sitting back on the settee with a cup of coffee, she reflected over the last few days, knowing her mother was on the brink of a new life.

Graham was the first to arrive home, obviously pleased to see his mother and hear the news about the flat. He told her he would be away at the weekend as he and his girlfriend were going to Wales for a few days. 'That should be nice this time of year,' said Gemma with a smile.

Zoe came through the door singing ten minutes later and threw her arms around her mother. 'It's good to have you back.'

Gemma brought her up to date.

'I'm having my driving lesson to-night,' Zoe informed her.

'Oh, what time?'

'7.15.'

'Oh right, then I had better see what is in the fridge for tea.'

'Oh Mum, I shall be staying at Pip's this week-end, her father is away again.'

'Brilliant!' exclaimed Gemma, walking towards the kitchen. 'It just wants your father to say he is away too and I might as well have stopped where I was.'

'Sorry Mum,' said Zoe.

'Oh well – I might appreciate a quiet weekend after all the running about I have been doing.'

Graham shrugged his shoulders.

Loud thumping and banging came from the kitchen, Zoe and Graham looked at each other. A moment later Gemma stormed into the room red-faced and looking angry. 'Hasn't anyone done any shopping while I've been away?' With quickened steps she walked over to the television and switched it off, leaving a complete look of surprise on Graham's face; he had only just switched it on.

Standing in front of them stern faced like a headmistress about to address the class for unruly behaviour, 'You are a hopeless bunch,' she began, 'I go away for a few days and the whole place falls apart. How do you see me? Someone who does the shopping, the cooking, the cleaning, washing and ironing keeping the place clean and ticking? Oh Mum will do that. That is Mum's job. You are hopeless. You all come in, eat the food I have cooked and NOT ONE of you, your Dad included, thought of restocking the fridge. Has anyone put a cleaner round the place? Or a duster, while I have been away – Oh no, that's Mum's job. I have not exactly been on holiday myself, driving my mother all over the place finding somewhere for her to live . . .' She stamped out of the room. ' I come home to this – I'm fed up with the lot of you! It's a wonder the kitchen sink is not full of dirty pots.' The bedroom door slammed behind her.

Silence hung about the room. Both sat motionless, almost afraid to speak to each other.

Robert's car could be heard drawing up outside. Two minutes later he appeared in the silent room. 'Am I in the right house?' He looked at both of them. 'Where is Mum?' Zoe pointed to the bedroom.

'Oh.' He realised things were not right. He quietly opened the bedroom door. Gemma was sitting on the bed crying.

'Can I help?' he said sitting beside her and putting his arms around her. In between sobs she told him how it should have been a happy occasion – telling him about the flat she had found for her mother – instead she had come home to an empty fridge. She felt a lack of support. 'Has anyone put a duster round the place or a cleaner?' she asked him. 'What am I – a workhorse?'

'Aye now that is not true, we all love you, don't upset yourself. Tell you what we will do. Forget tonight's meal, we will all go to that new place in Quorn. Do you fancy that? Call it a welcome home meal.'

She nodded her approval. He kissed her on the cheek and left her to tidy up.

Back in the lounge two very subdued young persons sat motionless and looked at him as he entered. 'Forget what happened just now, we are all going out for an evening meal.'

'But Dad . . .' Graham began. He was cut short.

'ALL going out for a meal, is that clear?' Robert said with some authority. 'You can ring your girlfriend and tell her you will see her about 8 o'clock.'

'Dad, I have a driving lesson just after seven,' Zoe said nervously.

'In that case you will not be with us, but Graham – YES.' He disappeared into the bathroom.

The next morning saw the household back onto an even keel again. Graham was out of the house before Robert or Zoe made an appearance, Gemma was busy in the kitchen when Robert arrived. Zoe was standing in front of the mirror paying attention to her pony tail hairstyle more than her breakfast.

'Does that look all right Mum?'

'Yes darling – going somewhere special?'

'Maybe.'

'Where does this one come from?'

'Syston . . . Works in his father's chemist shop near the memorial,' she turned and faced her father, 'and his name is Robert!' she laughed.

'I was thinking,' Robert said in between bites of his toast. 'Still want to go to the cottage, get a bit of sea air as I suggested before your mother decided to move house and take up your time?'

'When?'

'How about next week, starting on Saturday?'

'Suits me,' Zoe said, emerging from the bedroom, 'I can do some horseriding while I'm there, that is if the horses are still there, it has been years now.'

'About four years, Zoe,' said Gemma.

'Is it – Good Lord! Should know my exam results by then.' She looked in the mirror again as she passed. 'Right – I'm off.'

'Don't be too late back.'

'Don't worry, he is a gentleman, plays cricket for Syston Town.'

'So playing cricket makes him a gentleman does it?' said Robert.

'Ha ha, very funny,' she replied as she disappeared through the doorway.

The proposed holiday at the cottage had been put on hold following a telephone conversation from Gemma's mother. Her home in Chorley had been sold almost immediately it was put on the market but the purchasers wanted a quick completion of deeds. As they were prepared to pay the asking price there was little point in hanging about, so a hot line was set up between Gemma's mother and the agent for the flats. The result being; occupation of the flat would be available the following week.

'Don't worry Zoe,' Gemma said, 'I'll only be gone a few days, then we can go off to the cottage, Lord knows I'll need a break after this lot.'

Arriving at Chorley Gemma helped put the final small pieces into her car, closed the door of her home of many years behind her for the last time, and set off to the flat in a different area of Chorley with her excited mother beside her.

On arrival they were confronted by a series of tea-chests placed about the various rooms, delivered earlier by the removal people. The carpets had been fitted earlier but the first task was the bedroom. Although the curtains had not yet been delivered, it was essential they had somewhere to sleep.

After two days, obvious inroads had been made, and apart from the curtains still not delivered, the place was beginning to look like home.

Both were feeling the strain of emptying the contents of the tea-chests and arranging them about the flat.

'Mum,' said Gemma, 'let's go outside for a bit.'

'Why not,' was the reply, 'we've done the hard bit – we need a break.'

It was peaceful in the garden. There were people passing in the road but they could not be seen. It was a beautiful day, radiant with tall colourful flowers of different varieties adorning the flower beds. A heap of rubbish was burning in a corner of the garden, the smoke rising steadily in a final loveliness from earth to the sun.

The house was originally built for the owner of several mills in Shaw and Darwen in Lancashire. It had seen his family grow up there, witnessed weddings, funerals happiness and sorrow. Lack of interest by the sons of his family, together with death duties, saw the family fortune dwindle and the house fall into disrepair. Eventually it was bought by a senior surgeon from Manchester Royal Infirmary who restored it to its former glory, adding a large conservatory. The house heard the tragic news of the *Titanic* disaster, in which a distant cousin of the family was a survivor, living until he was 69 and dying in Somerset. It saw its sons go to war in France in 1914, one never to return. It witnessed victory parades, hunger strikes and the depression which followed, the General Strike of 1926. The solo flight of Amy Johnson to Australia and the disaster of the airship R101 over France. The unrest in the political world with the Blackshirts of Oswald Mosley, the rumblings in Europe, the rising of Nazism under Adolf Hitler in Germany and the war which followed in 1939. The re-building of cities afterwards, the space age – Man on the moon. The cold war with Russia, Vietnam, the Rivers of Blood speech by Enoch Powell on Immigration, the IRA bombings in England and Ireland. The closure of the coal mines, the decline of the steel and car industry. The Beatles, rock music, jet airliners, fast cars and motorways ... Now this grand house before them bought by the developers was about to enter the twenty-first century.

Somewhere in a tree a blackbird was in full song.

'Beautiful isn't it Mum?'

'Yes, fancy a cup of tea?'

FOURTEEN

Gemma had been back at 'Farcroft' a week after seeing her mother settle in at her new abode. Robert was delivering his last lecture at the end of the university year in Reading, having spent two days attending a conference on World Environment and Pollution. Zoe was finding life very demanding and was anxiously awaiting her exam results, horseriding with Pip and her new boyfriend Robert. Graham was rarely at home now the rugger season had finished, most week-ends he was away with his girlfriend.

Gemma found herself more in isolation watching her children grow up, carving out their own future, and her husband away on his many excursions. At times she felt very lonely, but this solitariness did not last long, as she turned her attention again to her piano playing as often as possible.

Zoe was now nineteen, tall and slim with long flowing blonde hair and her mother's good looks making her a confident, ambitious and self assured young lady. For months she had been taking driving lessons, this would complete her independence, and like Graham, she would move on.

Robert arrived home in a joyful mood and announced at the evening meal that he had no further commitments until the beginning of September.

'This means we can go to the cottage whenever we want.'

He looked round the table for some response – none came. 'Maybe I'll go on my own then,' he teased.

'No Dad,' said Zoe, 'I want to come but my exams results should be out by then, and I want to know how I've done.'

'You can telephone Graham. He will be working, he is not coming with us' Gemma added.

'No thank you,' Zoe snapped, 'I'd rather phone the college.'

'Do that then.'

'You could always leave a forwarding address,' suggested Robert. 'Anyway the main thing is, do you want to come with us? If so, let us fix a date.'

'Yes I want to come with you. It would be a change, sea air, riding on the beach, yes, great fun. Thanks Dad.'

The date was fixed for the second and third week in August.

Throughout the month of July, there had been little if any rain, with the weather forecast of no change in the near future. The threat of a hose-pipe ban was mooted. The road outside 'Farcroft' leading to Bradgate Park was very dry, dust covering the hedges and trees and dulling down any colour in the countryside, needing a good downpour to bring back the lustre. Clouds of dust rose each time a car passed, filling the air in the constant oppressive heat of day, making it difficult to breath.

Zoe was stretched out on a lounger on the lawn wearing a bikini top and shorts, counting the days when they would be in the cool sea breeze and wide open spaces.

Gemma came out of the kitchen carrying two coffees on a tray.

'Coffee Zoe?'

'Oooooh yes please.'

'Another hot day. Just think in a few days we shall be near the sea wherever we are on the island. We are really lucky to have a place by the sea, I'm looking forward to it, and I know your Dad is. We have not been there for such a long time. I shall take all the hot water bottles we have to air the beds and we shall take sleeping bags and our own pillows,' added Gemma, putting down the tray of coffee.

The final stages of packing were under way. Last minute instructions were given to Graham, now in charge of 'Farcroft'. He assured them not to worry, he could cope.

The last piece of luggage was pushed into the car boot accompanied with hugs and kisses as Robert sprung the car into life. Graham stood there as the car drove slowly away. A strange quietness wrapped round him before he entered the house.

The sun was still low in the East but all the signs for another hot day were evident. The sky was a pale cerulean blue with no breath of wind or cloud as Robert drove across country towards Melton Mowbray. At a small lay-by he pulled in.

'What's wrong?' asked Gemma.

'No panic' he answered, 'just a minor adjustment.' Unseen by the occupants he opened the boot and took out two 'L' plates, fixing one on the rear of the car, the other on the front. Returning to the car on the passenger side, he turned to Zoe, sitting in the rear seat. 'OK madam, get out and drive us.'

'WHAT? ME!'

'Yes, you CAN drive can't you?'

'Yes but . . .'

'No buts, just get in and drive.' He spent a few minutes explaining where everything was, then turning on the ignition Zoe pulled away very smoothly. Robert sat back, impressed by the way she handled the 2 litre Volvo. He put that down to horseriding; the beast obeying her every command. Feeling relaxed he said, 'Go through Oakham then onto the A1 north, stop at Scotch Corner for lunch.'

'OK!' she replied.

Confidently she overtook slower vehicles, tankers, caravans and large lorries, looking into her mirror with the assurance of a more experienced driver.

After lunch Zoe continued her driving, little was spoken as mile after mile slipped by. In the afternoon the Westmorland hills came into view in the West.

The temperature was now into the eighties but Zoe showed no sign of strain.

'Let me know when you have had enough,' said Robert, knowing full well what the answer would be!

'I'm OK thanks . . . why, do you want to drive?'

'ME? No! I'm quite happy being driven.'

The afternoon slipped by with the occasional glimpse of the sea through the trees on the right as they journeyed north. By late afternoon the first sight of Bamburgh Castle came into view, and close by Lindisfarne Castle perched on its rock of dolomite with the sea beyond and Farne Isles in the distance. Excitement sounded in Robert's voice. 'Just hope we have got the tide right,' he said peering through the window.

'Me too,' replied Zoe. 'If there is water on the road you drive, I might go off it.'

'You should be all right, just follow any other car going over.'

Arriving at Beal just before the causeway they came to a halt behind other vehicles lined up for the crossing.

As witnessed on many occasions, there is always someone short of patience. All eyes were now focused on a small white car moving slowly through the sea-water, ploughing the water before it as the driver risked the crossing. Deeper into the water at every yard progressed, the sea obviously inside the car by now, the driver stopped.

It looked foolish, a solitary car sitting in the sea with the water halfway up the doors, alone in a vast expanse of water.

'Hope he keeps his engine running,' said Robert. 'I have seen that so many times before – it's risking untold damage to the car.'

Half-an-hour later the traffic in front of them began to move steadily forward. Zoe drove with extreme care until they arrived outside the cottage.

Robert was the first out of the car saying, 'Thank you, driver!'

He stood looking at the cottage deep in his own thoughts. Zoe and her mother watched him taking in the whole scene. He found difficulty opening the old rotting wooden gate. The front garden was a tangled mass of thistles, nettles, tall grass, bramble and convolvulus, which had run riot in every direction. Bees were plentiful, busy working from flower to flower – some, hidden in the undergrowth, survivors of better days. The white paint on the window frames had departed long ago leaving the bare wood to the elements.

Holding back the bramble with one hand he moved slowly forward, hacking a path through the jungle-like undergrowth towards the side door. Inserting the key into the door he was surprised to find the door still tightly stuck fast. With one mighty heave with his shoulder the door yielded, releasing a blast of cold, dank air. Silence met him as he stepped inside. Like retracing steps back into the past he stood looking about him as he ventured further into the interior. It was a strange feeling. This was once his home. This was where he grew up with his parents. It was here he would return after his walk on the beach with a new collection of 'finds'. His mother would be in the kitchen preparing a meal, his father would be sitting in his favourite chair reading the newspaper with a pipe in his mouth.

'Are you coming in?' he called.

Without answering they both stepped inside, holding hands for re-assurance.

'Better open some doors and windows, get some fresh air in the place.'

'I never thought it would be like this,' Gemma said, looking around her.

'Me neither,' added Zoe.

'We will soon have the place looking like home. You start unpacking the car and I will start cleaning up,' said Robert taking off his jacket.

Zoe and Gemma went out into cool clean air and stood against the car, taking in deep breaths before unloading their things.

Both Gemma and Zoe squirmed as they entered the kitchen. Dead beetles lay in the sink together with a number of blowflies, cobwebs hung from every conceivable place, forming a thick heavy veil between the two taps and dangling like streamers from the light fitting. The curtains across the window were parched and faded, hanging in tatters. Thick layers of dust covered the flooring like a carpet, A dead starling lay in the hearth, a victim of a fall down the chimney, and the windows were tinted grey with layers of dust accumulated over time. The grandfather clock in the corner stood looking forlorn and neglected, covered in a blanket of yet more cobwebs.

Upstairs was much the same. The air smelled dank and cold, brought on by the thick stone walls of the cottage denying any penetration by the sunlight. Dark corners and crevices of the room concealed by tattered tapestries and fatigued draperies suggested that spiders, black beatles and other creepy-crawlies were now in residence.

Hot water bottles were brought in together with sleeping bags, food and drinks. Robert was busy shaking mats outside then applying the cleaner to them.

'We will soon have the place looking like home, then I will take you out for a meal,' he said in between gasps of air.

'I think a bath would be more apt,' said Zoe.

'That can be arranged too, later when the water has had time to heat up.'

Two hours later Robert stood in the middle of the room with his sleeves rolled up. Gemma looking dishevelled with black smudges on her face, and Zoe, more interested in her fingernails and breathing heavily, broke the silence. 'My God', she said, 'what a start to a holiday. Having driven you both here all the way to the sea, I feel I want to jump in it. Next time I think I will come by coach.'

'Sorry about that Zoe, I had no idea it would be as bad as that. Thank you both for all your help. Can I now declare Seawinds . . . open?'

Gemma and Zoe disappeared upstairs to the bathroom in preparation for the evening meal. Robert walked down the garden path, brushing aside the tall grass and bramble as he went. Thankfully the pile of lobster and crab pots, netting, buoys etc, had long gone. Ragweed, daisies, bugle and dock occupied a large part of the garden, with a few faded and wilted lupins and dahlias the sad remains of a family garden. At the lower end of the garden path, barely visible through the dense mass of weeds and grass, stood the remains of his father's boat. The once painted white hull was now looking shabby, its paint peeling off and the name *Northern Pride* barely readable. He stood for a moment deep in thought. Close by was the rough wooden cross his mother made for Butch. 'Good old Butch,' he thought, 'I miss you, I miss you both.'

He turned back towards the cottage, thinking how long it had been since he was here last. Since Mary's death they had made few visits. Life had changed, the children were growing up with their own interests taking priority over the cottage. His own happy childhood passed through his mind; the fishing trips with his son Graham; Zoe riding with her friend from the farm; his father's tragic death and the sudden unexpected death of Mary. He quickly turned his head away from the cottage and looked up to the sky as if wanting to shut out the memory of his guilt in the past with Jackie in that bedroom where he slept with Gemma his wife last night.

He was up and out early the next morning walking along the shoreline on an incoming tide feeling exhilarated, his hands deep into his pockets. The breeze ruffled his hair as he walked along looking for 'finds', a lifetime habit. The sun in the East was low on the horizon, offshore a small boat was moving up and down on the waves as the solitary figure on board was seen to be handling crab pots. Robert stood watching as gannets flew past him screeching. That could be my father, he thought. Eventually he heard the boat's engine start up and move away.

Cormorants sat on the rocks drying their outstretched wings. Oyster-catchers and avocets dug for food in the wet sand before him.

An hour later he returned to the cottage. Gemma was in the kitchen as he entered to the smell of coffee and toast 'Mmmm smells good,' he said, kissing her on the cheek. 'It's lovely out there.'

'See anyone you knew?'

'No – Just me and the birds. Oh, and a boat putting pots out.'

Zoe appeared from the bathroom rubbing her hair with a towel. 'You were out early,' she said.

'Didn't want to miss anything.'

'Did you miss anything?'

'No – saw the island come to life with a golden light in the East and a solitary fishing boat in the early morning light.'

'Sounds nice!' she teased.

'It was like poetry, beautiful.'

'Oh God, what have I started?'

Gemma put more toast on the table. 'I thought we might ring Jackie, tell her we are here, what do you think?'

'Sure,' said Robert. 'You can ring from the pub.'

'Oh I completely forgot we are not on the phone now. I think she likes coming here,' Gemma said.

'Why don't we all go over to Berwick? It would make a change,' replied Zoe. 'I would love to look round that place.'

'I'll see what Jackie says,' Gemma said, pouring out more coffee. 'I agree Berwick does look a nice place.'

Their first full day on the island was spent on the beach area towards the mound of hard dolerite rock which runs for 70 or 80 miles across the north of England. Perched on this rock stands Lindisfarne Castle, built to protect against the invading Scots. It lay in ruins until it was rebuilt by Sir Edwin Lutyens and made habitable.

Gemma had been in touch with Jackie, who was delighted they were on the island, and had arranged to meet them in two days' time giving them time to settle in.

The weather still remained unbearably hot, a few puffs of thin white cloud in a blue sky, with little breeze, incessant heat, dust thrown up at the slightest movement, plants withering and dying through lack of water. Prayers were said in the churches, asking for rain to save the crops. The situation was getting critical, water was now a precious commodity.

After the walk on the beach they returned to the cottage, sitting outside in the garden despite the weeds and bramble.

The following day saw them in Bamburgh. The weather was still hot; the sky cloudless with little breeze to relieve the monotony of the continuous searing heat.

Robert suggested a trip on the sea to the Farne Isles, a suggestion which both Gemma and Zoe agreed to immediately. 'Anything for a breath of fresh air,' said Zoe.

Out on the sea, with the speed of the boat and escape from the shelter of buildings the air was a welcome guest as it ruffled the hair of the people aboard.

'It's like going down memory lane,' said Robert, focusing his binoculars on the cliffs en route for the lighthouse. Puffins and cormorants sat watching them. A few bull seals basked in the hot sun, ever watchful as some slid gently into the sea. Kittiwakes, common and artic tern and a few lesser black backed gulls, with the accompanying 'whitewash' on the cliffs pointed out over the tannoy making everyone look in that direction amongst sniggers.

The remains of the old tower on Staple Island close by, used as a beacon in the time of Grace Darling's father and partly destroyed in a storm at the end of the eighteenth century, was now a sea of flowering campion, guillemots, razor-bills, oystercatchers and eider ducks.

A visit to the Grace Darling museum in Bamburgh seemed to complete the afternoon retracing steps of time gone by, where as a complete family they enjoyed the childish banter and laughs of delight as they came face to face with maritime history.

Feeling somewhat refreshed after the sea trip, a leisurely light meal in a nearby cafe was appreciated before setting off back to the cottage in the late afternoon.

Thankful the temperature had dropped a little as the day moved on, Robert decided to start making inroads on the weed surrounding the hull of Bert's boat and Butch's grave. Dressed only in shorts he chopped and tugged at the overgrowth of bramble and convolvulus, heaving at their stubborn roots reluctant to leave the ground. He was breathing fast and his brow covered with sweat, as the heavy clods of earth with the roots still clinging on finally gave way revealing dry brown earth beneath. So engrossed in this mammoth task he failed to see the storm clouds gathering behind him.

Gently at first the raindrops fell about him, making him look up to the sky where he saw the clouds darkening above him. In the distance faint rumblings of thunder. The noise of rain falling on the large dock leaves in the garden made him decide to go indoors. Approaching the cottage doorway the rain increased to a downpour in a matter of seconds, making him run the last few steps. A flash of forked lightning ripped through the sky, followed by an earsplitting crack of thunder. He stood in the doorway watching the sky, the rain now beating down with tremendous force, hitting the baked hard surface, rebounding back looking like darts, leaving streams of water running like miniature rivers forming pools of water on the brown clay earth. The clouds seemed to get lower, black and angry edged with a reddish tinge. The wind speed increased in ferocity, bending bushes at alarming angles as its roots held on desperately to the ground.

'Don't stand there!' called Gemma.

'It is all right Gemma, it's been years since I saw a good storm over the sea.'

Forked lightning mixed with sheet lightning lit the sky, the ground shook with the violent claps of thunder. Torrents of rain now turned to hale, white balls of frozen water like small garden peas bombarded the ground then rolled into groups amassing together in the low parts of the ground looking like snow. The clouds above now formed a towering cumulonimbus top so high, composed mainly of ice. Strong gust of winds at almost gale force rocked the garden fences. Plant pots, watering cans and anything not secured was moved with considerable force, After fifteen minutes or so the centre of the storm shifted.

Inky black and purple sky rent by rolls of lightning, towering clouds and sudden cracks of thunder is a dramatic experience, leaving one in awe at the immense power of nature. Robert stood taking it in, remembering the days in his youth when he had witnessed such scenes. He also remembered the storm which cost his father his life. He looked down the garden path towards the wrecked hull of the boat, all that remained of a man's life. Now after the torrential rain it stood isolated in a large pool of water. The lightning grew fainter and fainter till it was only a flash of a distant blade. The thunder growled even further away. The wind lessened as if exhausted. The bushes ceased to tremble as the clouds dispersed and the copper sun appeared in the west, slowly melting away. Soon the island would be ready to sleep.

A few white clouds on an almost clear sky reflected in the many pools of water left lying about the following morning, with a gentle breeze. It was the day of Jackie's visit. The rain-soaked trees and bushes still dripping after the storm of yesterday made everywhere smell fresh, and the conditions after the oppressive heat were bearable once more.

Zoe had gone to the farm further in the village, Gemma was busy making the place look presentable in readiness for her visitor. Robert was restless. It was too wet to do anything in the garden, and he was too excited at seeing Jackie again – yet nervous after a long time of absence, which left him in doubt. How would he react? How would she affect him? The fire of desire had lain low over the years, but soon she would be near him again. He looked forward to seeing her with mixed feelings. How would she feel after a long absence? He would soon find out. Low tide was around 5 pm.

Just after 5.15 pm Jackie's car drew up outside the cottage. Robert saw her approach as he looked through the window and caught his breath. She looked stunning. Elegant as ever, fashionably dressed, her trim figure and shapely legs moved gracefully down the garden path towards the door. Gemma opened it and instantly threw her arms around her, hugging her tightly. 'It's so good to see you again!'

'It is good to see you Gemma, it has been a long time,' replied Jackie. She turned and saw Robert standing close by. 'And how is my favourite boyfriend?'

Slightly stunned at that opening remark he put on a brave face saying, 'I'm fine thanks Jackie.' The two women sat on the settee, Robert sat in an easy chair opposite. The conversation soon turned to Jackie's domestic situation, showing no sign of sadness and pulling no punches. Robert had heard it years before but now the truth of her phoney wedding and marriage was about to be made public. She went on to tell how her husband, John rarely came home, and how he took little interest in his daughter Roslin. Gemma sat back slightly amazed at what she was hearing, but Jackie was now speaking openly and frankly, clearly wanting to bring attention to her lonely life. She shifted slightly on the settee, revealing more of her shapely legs for the benefit of Robert sitting opposite.

From the conversation he learned that Roslin was now in a steady relationship with a man from Berwick, working in The Royal Bank of Scotland, and it was only a matter of time until she would leave her home, leaving her mother completely on her own.

'Hi Jackie!' came a voice from the doorway, making all heads turn in that direction. Zoe walked over to Jackie who was sitting on the settee. 'Been here long?'

'Half an hour or so. Did you get a ride?'

'No – not today. But we are going out early on the beach.'

Robert was feeling out of the conversation and decided to go down the garden path with a feeling that Jackie was already mapping out a future with him. He felt uncomfortable, his own guilt was beginning to trouble him. He had heard enough.

He stood looking at the area where he had been working yesterday before the storm. The warm sun had dried most of the surface water and fallen leaves, and the ground beneath him was getting firmer again. A slight haze hung over the sea. The air felt fresh and salty after the deluge. He stood taking in deep breaths of air for fifteen minutes or so before returning to the cottage to the sound of loud laughter.

'Sounds like a good joke?' he said, entering and sitting in the easy chair again, as Jackie looked at him, moving her legs for him.

'Jackie was just telling us of the time she had a date and went to the hairdresser in the afternoon,' Gemma said laughing, 'some weeks ago now. She had accepted an invitation to a dinner by some sales rep in the hairdressing trade.' Gemma, still laughing, continued. The thought of Jackie out with another man unsettled him, he shifted uneasily in the chair as if he had heard enough. 'It was a wet windy day,' said Gemma. 'When she had finished having her hair done, she looked in the mirror and was satisfied with what she saw,' she chuckled again, 'went out of the salon door at exactly the same time as a lorry splashed through a large pool of rainwater in the gutter and splashed all over her. She went back into the salon with black smudges over her face and her hair in a mess. The drain outside the shop had become blocked.'

'And that was a joke?' he said with a note of sarcasm.

'Well not at first, but we can see the funny side of it now.'

'Oh come on dad, where is your sense of humour?'

Both Gemma and Jackie sat laughing. 'You will have to excuse dad,' said Zoe, 'he never had his Wheaty Puffs this morning!'

'Leave it Zoe,' cut in Gemma. 'Why don't we all go for a short walk?'

It was more of a ramble than a walk, the three women walking together leaving Robert apart from them as they reached the end of the cottages in view of the castle and sea. Sheep were grazing on the slopes of the mound in the shadow of the castle, the sea beyond was tranquil blue. White sails of yachts glided along its surface with gulls wheeling above. The air was fragrant, the few clouds earlier had given way to mares-tails stretching as far as the eye could see, the grass beneath their feet barely moved.

'Did you hear Robert? Jackie wants us to go over to her next week. What do you think?'

'Fine by me, see what the tide is doing.'

Gemma and Zoe went walking in the village the next morning. A sea mist hung about making everything dismal and out of focus. Both referred to Jackie's visit, obviously enjoying her company, and thought it sad that her marriage had faltered. 'She is so attractive,' said Gemma, 'I wonder if she will go out to live with John if Roslin leaves home?'

'Doubt it by the sound of things,' replied Zoe. 'Oh look, there is a phone box.'

'I'll be in that shop while you make your phone call.'

Gemma was looking through the display of view cards, having already purchased a bottle of local mead from the general stores when Zoe burst in. 'Mum I've passed!'

'Oh jolly good, Zoe, congratulations!'

Robert was working in the garden clearing away the tangle of weeds around Bert's old boat and Butch's wooden cross, a task interrupted by the storm. The sound of voices made him look up. 'Dad' shouted Zoe, 'I've passed my exams – I've got my City and Guilds!'

'Well done, congratulations, that is great!' He walked towards her with arms outstretched which she readily fell into, both hugging each other.

'We thought while we were out we would give the college a ring.'

'So what happens now?' asked Robert.

'Carry on as before. I should get a raise in wages now I am fully qualified. Then perhaps I might open my own salon!' She danced, waving her arms about in the air.

'When will that be?'

'Don't know – I need a bit more practical experience and a course in management, then I'll see.'

FIFTEEN

The smell of the sea on a fresh morning breeze coming from the north east reached them; as the car was slowly driven across the causeway trying to avoid as much seawater left behind by the receding tide as possible. Cumulus cloud had gathered blotting out the sun at this early hour giving a sharp nip in the air A few yards in front of him splashing through the pools was a black pick-up truck lurching from side to side stacked with boxes of crabs. Robert kept a safe distance, understanding the importance of catching the early wholesale market, a situation his own father would have experienced.

Zoe sat in the rear of the car looking out at the vast expanse of glittering mud, a regular feeding ground for the many types of sea birds. Along the causeway stood birdwatchers with binoculars or telescopes on tripods trained on the screaming, wheeling mass of this haven for birds stretching from Lindisfarne to Budle Bay.

'Make the most of it, Zoe,' said Robert. 'You have only a week left then it is back to the Midlands.'

'You mean civilisation don't you?'

'Why do you say that?'

'Well it is nice, for a change, but I miss the big shops, the busy streets, the people, all that sort of thing.'

'Missing the boyfriend, are we?'

'NO, not just that, I think it is called LIFE.'

'But this IS life Zoe,' Robert replied. 'Nature, birds, weather, the sea. True life, not your artificial bustling busy so-called life, teeming with people who haven't got the time of day to stop and look around them. Some have not the time to breathe, making money is more important.'

'Oh yes, it has been a change after all that hot weather, but give me the town anytime.'

* * *

Jackie greeted them as they entered her house with hugs and kisses. The last few months had been lonely for her. She had few friends in Berwick despite having lived in this house for great number of years. Few thought of calling. Her weekly trip to the supermarket or hairdresser had become the highlight of her week. She read a lot and had become an expert with crosswords. Other than that, the TV or radio had become her companion in her boring life.

Today was different. She was exhilarated almost to the point of bursting into song. She loved Robert deeply and secretly, guarding those precious moments they had shared together. She knew he had loved before with Linda before marrying Gemma, but for her something had happened for the first time in her life. That miracle, that magic, that incredible loveliness, for such a short period of time. Now once more he stood before her in the hallway, and she desperately wanted to run into his arms, but the situation forbade it. Only a few days ago at the cottage he seemed aloof, distant, was it an act?

Robert was also finding it difficult, the smell of her perfume filled his nostrils as she stood near him, reminding him of how in the past moments of fulfilment, time had stood still. As they walked along the hall to the lounge, he observed the way she taunted him as she moved, touching his arm whenever she got near to him or as she made a point in a conversation. The frustration was with both of them. The escape came when it was suggested they go out for a meal.

He sat next to her in the car as they drove into Berwick, the strong fragrant aroma of her perfume percolating though the car was having a devastating effect on him. The conversation as they travelled towards Berwick was mainly of historical interest or architecture. Inwardly he had hoped that Jackie had put their affair out of mind, but Jackie had other ideas. At every opportunity she touched him on the arm or made physical contact with him, giving him a look which he had recognised from the past. During the meal he was finding it hard to keep a low profile, answering questions, being polite and generally putting on a brave face, but inwardly he was fighting. Fighting his own desires and conscience. With this struggle within he was missing out on the jokes, the amusing stories and comical incidents.

He felt like an outsider, his mind wandering off in different directions. All he could do was sit and listen to their happy chatter above the clatter of knives and forks.

After the meal the conversation flagged in contrast to the earlier mood. Jackie came to the rescue, sensing the awkward lull, by suggesting she took them on a tour of the town. It was no new adventure for Robert. During his schooldays Berwick had always attracted him, and with its shops, museums, art galleries, this fifteenth-century town with its ramparts was for Zoe and Gemma a real treat. Stopping at various points looking at the wide River Tweed with its ships and numerous birds wheeling around, Zoe pointed out that her father always went the opposite way when they came to the cottage, going to places like Bamburgh, Seahouses and Alnwick.

At that Jackie suggest that Zoe spend a few days with her before she went back. Zoe was overjoyed, Gemma agreed and Robert nodded his approval.

Parking her car adjacent to a large attractive park, Jackie suggested that as the weather was pleasant they should walk there, telling them that when the weather was warm after a shopping trip she often sat there to relax. She cleverly manoeuvred herself to be walking alongside Robert as they strolled slowly along through the flower filled park. Striking colours skillfully set out, trees and bushes in full bloom made an idyllic setting for a small lake and graceful swans and moorhens. Passing a pair of young lovers sitting on a bench in a tight embrace, Jackie took the opportunity of giving Robert a quick glance of approval. Further along a vacant seat beckoned. Again Jackie made sure she sat next to him, making contact with him by pressing her legs against him as they sat down. To the amusement of everyone a very small black and white puppy belonging to the lady on the next seat was rolling about on the floor playing with its lead and yelping when its head got entangled.

'I think I have fallen in love with Berwick,' Zoe said. 'It's clean, interesting and different, I wouldn't mind living here.'

'Yes it is quite nice here, but then I've lived here a long time so I am biased,' Jackie agreed. 'But your place is back home where your work is.'

'The world is my oyster now I have qualifications, I can move anywhere I like.'

'Funny you should say that, Zoe,' broke in Jackie. 'My hairdresser is about 33 or 35 years old, she has been married for some time now and wants to start a family, but says she could not cope with a baby and running her business, so she could be looking for a buyer soon.'

'Ooooh sounds good, just what I am looking for!'

'There is a two bedroom flat above – all very modern.'

'But,' said Gemma, 'you need experience in management first, bookkeeping, ordering stock, that sort of thing, and how to run a business.'

Robert remained silent. He felt her thigh push against him as she applied more pressure in this tight situation. She made an adjustment to her dress giving her a chance to touch his hand. His mouth went dry, making him fidget until he could no longer stay seated. Standing up he stretched his legs and walked about.

'Getting restless are we?' Jackie teased.

'Just a touch of cramp,' he answered.

'Well you have seen our park, what about a cup of tea back home?'

On the way back to Lindisfarne Zoe confessed to liking Jackie, she was fashionable, attractive and well spoken, why then did her husband not relate to her anymore? Why did he not take any notice of his daughter Roslin?

'That my dear is the sixty-four thousand dollar question,' Gemma replied. Robert refrained from commenting.

The sun was already going down as they neared the causeway. A few birds remained gathering the last scraps of food before the tide rushed in denying them further access. Small craft alongside the causeway were leaning at varying angles, also awaiting the tide to feel water beneath them again. Gemma and Zoe talked between themselves, recalling some of the more amusing and interesting moments involving Jackie. Robert kept quiet. Feelings for her had stayed dormant over the past few years, but seeing her again had rekindled the fire within him, recalling the happy times they had both shared. The day it snowed when they lunched together after his father's inquest. That day in Spring, the reddened sunset. The clear blue sky, the amber light, the cool cold air clear and crystal, her birthday dinner and the dance until midnight afterwards. The first time they made love, the love which lasted only a little while perhaps was more than some humans experienced in a lifetime.

Arriving back at the cottage, Zoe was thrilled with the idea of spending a few days with Jackie in Berwick. 'I'll see if Connie will go riding tomorrow as I won't have many more chances.'

Gemma put the kettle on for hot drinks. Robert made his way up to his old room upstairs and stood looking out of the window towards the castle in the fading light. A pale half-moon was low on the horizon but he could clearly make out the craters and seas on its surface. Scanning his eyes round the island – his island – memories flooded back to him of his carefree childhood days combing the beach for shells, stones and unusual objects.

That night he lay awake for some time – Jackie had re-entered his life.

During the days which followed Zoe had met up with Connie from the farm and was out riding most mornings along the beach. Connie was impressed with Zoe's skill at riding and admired her success at the recent horse show. Robert spent most of his time clearing and burning garden rubbish, with a huge bonfire sending up clouds of thick swirling smoke into the atmosphere. Gemma spent the morning tidying up and keeping the place respectable, and in the afternoon she and Robert would walk either along the beach or towards the castle, calling at the local for a drink and light meal. Jack Mason was a regular visitor, and between them they covered many interests, talking well into the afternoon.

The appointed hour for Zoe to meet Jackie was fast approaching, a prospect Robert looked forward to with mixed emotions, knowing that one gets fragments of happiness only for a brief time. As one gets older those moments get fewer, but REAL happiness, not scraps, where life is wonderful, harmonious and complete. Realistically Jackie was forbidden fruit, she was married. He too was a married man, sharing his life with his two children and his wife Gemma whom he loved dearly, but somehow not with the same passion. Since his closeness and passionate affair with Jackie, Gemma was not enough. He craved for the same fulfillment with the same insatiable desire of passionate love he had experienced with Jackie. After Linda's death in the Chinese earthquake, his life was turned upside down, he was lost, confused in his mind. Sometimes he wondered if Gemma suspected things were not quite right, but she never probed into his thoughts.

An ear splitting roar shattered the quiet peaceful day as two Javelin fighter planes flew low over the island, making him look up. The price we pay for peace, he thought. No wonder farmers complained of the effect of low flying aircraft had on the cattle in their fields.

To Zoe it seemed as if the appointed day for her to meet Jackie would never arrive. Despite her daily rides with Connie, the highlight of the holiday would be spending that time with Jackie. Tuesday was the day she would be taken over to Berwick, but Zoe had already spent the week-end packing and was ready to go.

Robert had already said sarcastically, 'Can't wait to get away from us . . .'

'Oh for goodness sake Robert, if Jackie wants her to stay a few days with her, why shouldn't she? I know if I had the chance I would jump at it.'

At that remark he suddenly got out of the chair and stormed out of the cottage, slamming the door behind him.

A seething rage had built up inside him as he walked towards the harbour. A gentle breeze had sprung up, ruffling the grass before him. Cumulus clouds were building up over the sea, with a drop in temperature. The weather pattern of the long hot run had changed since the storm. Distant thunder rumbled and the ominous sound of waves breaking against the breakwaters onto the shore could put a damper on Zoe's stay in Berwick.

The day to take Zoe across the causeway arrived with a steady drizzle, which accompanied them all the way to Jackie's front door just before 2.00 pm. Excitement filled the air with quick chatter. After a cup of tea it was a quick turn around before the tide changed, and by 4.00 pm Robert and Gemma were back in the cottage.

The following morning Jackie took Zoe shopping in Berwick, visiting the town centre, stopping at the bookshops, music shops, fashionable boutiques and cafes. A delighted and excited Zoe was full of admiration for Jackie, sharing an interest in fashion and music. This was a young girl's idea of a holiday. The town had a pulse, there was life here, it had pace and it excited. The island was good to relax in, you felt free, but after a while you looked for something more, and Berwick had that something for Zoe.

Turning from the main shopping area into a side street Jackie explained to Zoe, 'This is where my hairdresser is. I'll introduce you.'

The salon's interior was tastefully set out in modern decor with tall potted plants and large ornate mirrors. A row of washbasins and backwash basins occupied one side of the salon. A row of six hood dryers and magazine racks stretched along the far wall. There were plenty of cupboards and counter space, heated towel racks and sterilising cabinets.

Two young girls were busy attending clients sitting in two of the chairs while a third person was under one of the hood dryers reading a magazine. A tall attractive woman appeared from looking in a cupboard, 'Hello Jackie. Quite a surprise!'

'Hello Sue,' replied Jackie. 'Meet a friend of mine's daughter, Zoe. She is staying with me for a few days.'

Sue Palmer nodded towards Zoe.

'Zoe has just passed her City and Guilds Certificate in hairdressing.'

'Oh well done – now you are looking for a job?'

'Not really. I am working part-time at the moment back home.'

'And that's not all. She is a very accomplished horserider, having just won a medal at the Burleigh horse show.'

'My, you are a clever one! You should talk to Tanya over there, she is mad on horseriding,' Sue said, turning and pointing to a slim tall girl dressing out a client's hair.

Tanya Meadows was roughly Zoe's age, tall and slim with short black hair. Her father had bought her a horse for her eighteenth birthday which she kept at her home farm near Wooler, a few miles away.

'How long are you here for?' asked Sue.

'I go back on Sunday.'

'Oh that's a pity, but do drop in next time you come.'

'I most certainly will.' Turning towards Tanya, Zoe said, 'Perhaps we could arrange a ride sometime?'

'I'll look forward to that,' was the reply.

On the way back from the salon the conversation was about hairdressing, horses and the friendly atmosphere in the salon. 'It's just what I'm looking for, nice town near the river, living accommodation, what more could a girl ask for?'

'Is that what you want?'

'Dad's idea really. Get your experience, then branch out on your own, be your own boss.'

'Perhaps he is right. I'll keep my ears and eyes open.'

'Thanks – if only!' Zoe sank back in the seat and closed her eyes.

'Would you consider moving up here then?'

'Oh yes,' Zoe answered. 'It's not too far from my gran in Chorley, or to the cottage in Lindisfarne.'

'That is true,' Jackie replied, seeing the possibility of seeing more of Robert if all went well.

SIXTEEN

Sunday morning on the island began windy and raining with a heavy overcast sky. The forecast was for continuous heavy rain and winds reaching gale force at times. Not the kind of day for making the many trips to and from the car with luggage and bedding ready for the journey back home. The tide would be down at 3.00 pm. The pick-up point with Jackie and Zoe was the turn off for Belford on the A1 at 3.45 pm. With weather in this mood there would be little time for lengthy goodbyes in the transferring of the passenger.

By midday the packing was completed, checks were made in the cottage, all that remained now was the tide to be low enough to cross, and that would be another three hours.

Robert stood looking out of the window with the rain falling like a waterfall beneath a leaden sky. 'What a day to travel, we should have gone yesterday.'

'Then you would have deprived Zoe of going to the theatre last night,' replied Gemma.

Few people passed by the window that morning, those that did were huddled in their coats, the collars turned up, and sullen looks reflecting their feelings of despair or utter boredom evident in the way they walked with shoulders hunched, head pushed forward, hands deep in their pockets, looking like the matchstick men in a Lowry painting.

Robert smiled to himself at his astute observation.

By 1.30 pm they were both getting restless. Gemma had read all the reading matter available. Robert lay on the bed in his old room resting before the long drive back, occasionally looking out of the window at the incessant rain obliterating his view of the castle and surrounding area of HIS island.

'Fancy a cup of tea? last of the milk,' Gemma called upstairs.

'Yes please,' came the answer, Robert raising himself off the bed and walking slowly downstairs.

Back at Jackie's house the scene was much the same. Zoe was packing upstairs, Jackie was preparing a light lunch with the radio playing country and western music.

Suddenly there was an interruption on the programme with a weather warning about conditions east of the Pennines.

'Oh dear Zoe,' said Jackie, calling upstairs, 'looks like you are in for a rough ride.'

'Why, what's the matter?'

'Torrential rain and gale force winds, widespread flooding, some minor roads closed, police redirecting traffic down the east of England.'

Zoe appeared with her suitcase. 'What a day to travel. I know one thing, Dad won't let me drive back.'

'I should think not. Come on let's eat.'

Just before 3.45 pm Jackie drew the car to a stop at the pre-arranged place on the A1. That short journey from Berwick with the windscreen wipers on fast and headlights on with spray from passing cars was as far as she wanted to drive on this treacherous day. Sitting in the layby talking, Jackie did not envy Robert's drive home in weather like today, with the latter part after nightfall, but Robert was adamant about getting back for Monday morning.

Sitting watching the cars passing in both directions throwing up cascades of spray and large lorries appearing like ghosts through a grey shroud made Zoe remark, 'It is going to be one hell of a drive for dad. I'm glad I'm not driving.'

Ten minutes passed. The sound of a car horn made them both turn round to see headlights pulling up behind them. Jackie was the first out of the car with a newspaper covering her head, Zoe followed with Robert getting out of his car to take Zoe's luggage and put it in the boot. A very quick goodbye, kisses thrown from the windows and frantic waving of arms, Jackie returned to her car and watched them drive away in a cloud of spray, then turned and made for home.

After three and a half hours of concentrated driving Robert announced he was stopping at the next service station. The light of day was already fading fast as he drew up at the service station with a sigh of relief. This welcome break was to recover from eye strain and to escape the constant appraisal of Jackie. It was apparent she had made great inroads of influence into Zoe's life.

Inside the warm, well lit cafeteria they sat with coffee and sandwiches, while through the large windows the rain ran down in a constant sheet of running water, the view beyond blurred. Robert sat with eyes closed preparing himself for the next encounter with the elements. There was still a very long way to go . . .

Above the constant noise of plates being rattled, the low conversation and the laughter of children, the wailing sound of a siren made everyone turn towards the window.

'Some poor devil in an accident in this lot.'

'I'm not surprised,' said Gemma, finishing off her coffee.

'Right' said Robert, 'I'll just go to the toilet then we are off.'

The monotonous rhythmic sound of the windscreen wipers on fast and the warm interior gave a false impression of security. Robert sat motionless, peering through the rain soaked windscreen with eyes wide open. The incessant rain hammering on the roof of the car with loud ferocity, dazzling lights reflected off the wet road of oncoming traffic, together with the occasional buffeting on the car in the very strong wind stretched his concentration to the limit. Gemma sat looking out of the side window watching the spray being thrown up. Zoe was reading a magazine on the back seat. No one spoke.

Most cars were happy to proceed at 35–40 mph. Some sped past in a reckless dash, throwing up even more water. Through the rain-covered windscreen Robert could just make out the vague shape of an oil tanker with its many lights on. The tanker appeared to slow down somewhat, giving Robert the chance to overtake and escape its spray. Unknown to him, further in front two cars were swerving across the road, forcing following cars to do likewise. Robert brought his car alongside the tanker in the instant the driver of the tanker braked, causing it to jack-knife on the wet surface and hit the side of Robert's car with great force, spinning it round like a child's toy smashing against the central barrier facing the opposite direction. The two cars immediately behind had little chance of avoiding them and ploughed into Robert's, finishing up in a pile on the roadside in a heap of twisted metal. The air was full of screams, with orders being shouted from following drivers offering assistance as they sped towards the trapped victims.

Amongst the wreckage of twisted cars, three cows were running aimlessly about the road.

* * *

Sometime the following day Robert slowly opened his eyes to a strange environment. His vision was blurred as he turned his head with great difficulty and began to focus on the ceiling. He was in a bed surrounded by a flower patterned curtain. Beyond the curtain he could hear muffled voices – His mind in turmoil forced an involuntary movement, alerting a nurse standing outside the curtain. 'Ah, so you have woken up,' a young attractive nurse said, pulling the curtains apart. She was roughly the same age as Zoe, dressed in a blue uniform with a white headband.

'Where am I?' he whispered.

'You are perfectly safe, don't worry. You are in hospital.'

'What happened?'

'I'll tell the doctor you are awake – don't worry.' She disappeared through the screen.

Lying looking up at the ceiling after the nurse had gone he tried to piece together the events as far as he could remember. It was raining heavily – he could remember that – he was driving his car . . . What happened next was a complete blur of sounds, breaking glass, crunching metal, debris flying, spinning round as if in fairground – then nothing. Nothing that is until he opened his eyes again and the young nurse was standing before him accompanied by a doctor in a white coat and a more senior nurse.

'Hello,' greeted the doctor. 'How do you feel?'

'Where am I? What happened?'

The doctor threw a glance towards the senior nurse. 'There was an accident, a big one on the A1 last night, a lot of people were injured.'

'What about my wife and daughter?' broke in Robert. 'They were with me.'

'I don't know about that but we will find out for you. First what about you? When they brought you in last evening we saw that your right leg had been injured so we put a splint on for the time being until we get you to the X-ray department. You have also done some damage to your pelvis, in the meantime you have a neck-brace on just in case you may have done some damage up there caused by whiplash.'

Slowly Robert put his hand down the bed and felt the splint on his right leg.

'Our job is to get you fit again, we will see where your wife and daughter are.' The doctor smiled down at him. 'The nurse will want to take your name and things like that, think you are up for it?'

'I'll be OK.'

'See you again then.' He disappeared through the curtain.

He lay back on his pillow, his mind in turmoil with the uncertainty of not knowing what happened to Gemma and Zoe. If he moved a sharp pain shot down his leg. How had it come to this? One moment he was driving the car with Gemma beside him and Zoe in the rear, the next moment all hell was let loose, he vaguely remembered a loud bang on the side of the car which left him spinning out of control – then nothing. His right hand was bandaged, with his left hand he could feel the plasters on his face and the brace about his neck, but his main concern was his right leg.

Two blue uniformed attendants entered the ward pushing a tea trolley. Each occupant of a bed was given a cup of tea with the usual chat and joke. Eventually the curtain was opened slightly and a smiling face appeared. 'Fancy a cuppa?'

'Please.'

'You are new here aren't you?'

'I suppose I am really but I don't feel very new at the moment.'

'You are in good hands here. Were you in that crash yesterday?'

'Yes – so was my wife and daughter, and I don't know what has happened to them.'

'I'll see what I can find out as I go round. Drink your tea . . .'

That morning the news broke on the television, radio, and headlines in the morning newspapers the headlines ran reporting the accident.

COWS CAUSE HAVOC ON THE A1
3 KILLED AND MANY INJURED AS COWS RUN AMOK IN TRAFFIC
WAS IT NEGLIGENCE OR VANDALISM?

TODAY POLICE ARE CONDUCTING ENQUIRIES INTO THE ESCAPE OF THREE COWS ONTO THE BUSY A1 LAST EVENING IN ATROCIOUS DRIVING CONDITIONS. COWS BELONGING TO 'FIELD HOUSE FARM' NEAR BARNBY MOOR ESCAPED FROM THEIR ENCLOSURE ONTO THE BUSY ROAD CAUSING DEATH AND DESTRUCTION.

3 KILLED AND SEVERAL INJURED, A TANKER JACK-KNIFED TRAPPING A CAR AGAINST THE CENTRAL RESERVATION BARRIER. THE OCCUPANTS WERE CUT FREE BY THE FIRE BRIGADE, CARS PLOUGHED INTO EACH OTHER CAUSING SERIOUS INJURIES. VICTIMS WERE TAKED TO NEARBY

WORKSOP AND RETFORD HOSPITALS. THE EXACT CAUSE OF THE ACCIDENT IS NOT YET KNOWN, BUT PASSING MOTORISTS EARLIER REPORTED SEEING TWO YOUTHS ON THE GRASS EMBANKMENT NEAR THE SPOT. A HELPLINE HAS BEEN SETUP . . .

Back at 'Farcroft' in Leicestershire Graham had expected his parents back around midnight, but dismissed that idea when he saw the state of the weather. Thinking they had delayed their departure until arriving home from work at the end of the day, he learned of the disaster on the six-o'clock news. Three killed, it said. Who were the three? Panic seized him. He quickly phoned the helpline which failed to subdue his inner feelings, leaving him in no doubt that he had to go to Worksop.

Graham appeared at his father's bedside accompanied by a nurse, having driven non-stop when he realised his parents were in that crash. Robert was lying with his eyes closed, his head back on the pillow when the nurse stopped at his bedside.

'Good God!' said Graham.

The sight of his father with a heavily plastered leg on traction, his right hand bandaged and his face covered with plasters and wearing a neck-brace, shocked him.

'Is that your father?' Asked the nurse.

'Yes, oh yes,' answered Graham.

'In that case we had better tell him you are here.'

She moved over to the lifeless form and whispered in his ear, 'Dr Watts – your son is here. Wake up.' She touched his arm; he stirred slightly.

Slowly he opened his eyes. 'There you are doctor, your son is here.'

'Hi Dad,' said Graham, stepping forward.

With a slight movement of his head and a half smile Robert responded in a weak voice, 'Glad you have come.'

'How bad is it ?' asked Graham.

The nurse butted in, 'Leg broken in two places, a bit out of your pelvis, a few cuts and bruises, not too bad really.'

'How are Mum and Zoe?' asked Robert, turning slightly towards Graham.

'Don't know, I've only just arrived. What happened?'

'All I can remember is – I was driving the car in the rain and a large tanker hit me in the side and spun me round and banged me against the central barrier – that's all I know.' He shifted slightly in the bed and winced with pain.

'In the papers this morning and on TV it mentions three cows were on the road.'

'COWS – I don't know anything about cows. It all happened so quickly.' He moved again in the bed in pain. 'I'm worried about Mum and Zoe, see what you can find out.'

'I will in a minute. Are you in much pain?'

'A bit – at least I'm alive.'

'According to the papers it was quite a pile up.'

The conversation was interrupted when two policemen entered with a staff nurse. They looked at Graham then at the heavily bandaged and plastered Robert with his leg in traction.

'Hello,' said one of the policemen, 'don't move.' Turning towards Graham, 'Are you a relation?'

'It's my father, I've only just got here.'

'Then you were not involved.'

'No. I was at home.'

'We have a few questions to ask if you don't mind.'

'That's OK, I'll take myself off and come back later.'

Graham left the bedside and approached the reception desk at the end of the ward. A seated nurse was busy sorting out a number of blue files. Looking up she greeted him with a smile. 'Can I help you?'

'Hello,' he started, 'I've just driven from Leicestershire to see my dad who is in this ward, he was involved in the crash yesterday, the police are with him now but my mother and sister were also with him in the car, could you please tell me where they are?'

'I'll see what I can find out.'

Graham moved away from the desk while the young nurse telephoned explaining the situation. Finally replacing the receiver she said, 'Dr Wainwright will see you, he knows more about it.' Ten minutes passed. Through the swing doors a small middle-aged man appeared and approached the nurse at the desk. Then turning, he looked at Graham.

'Mr Watts?'

Graham swung round. 'Yes.'

The doctor approached holding out his hand and smiled. They shook hands and the doctor led him outside the ward. 'Have you come far?'

'Leicestershire.'

'Nice county, Whitwick Monastery, Copt Oak, Shepshed ... My brother retired out there – Markfield – is that right?'

'Yes, Markfield. Not very far from where we live.'

'Oh really, where is that?'

'Near to Rothley and Bradgate Park.'

'Beautiful round there. Ah, here we are.' They stopped outside a row of curtained off wards.

The doctor approached the end portion and disappeared through it. Two minutes later he reappeared. 'Now describe your sister to me.'

'She is nineteen, blonde, slim ...'

'OK. Now, this person may be your sister. We have someone here but we do not know who she is. She is in a coma. Want to have a look?'

Graham's mouth went dry. He nodded his head and weakly said, 'Yes.'

'Follow me.'

Graham entered the room nervously and saw a still, pale figure with tubes inserted into her mouth held in place with plasters. An inverted bottle on a stand nearby supplied a liquid into her arm. On the wall, a screen registered an illuminated graph giving off a faint bleep every second which a young nurse sat watching for any change in tone. Graham moved over to the bedside and looked down at the face of his sister with her long blonde hair lying on the pillow. He gently touching her face.

The doctor stood beside him. 'I take it this is your sister?' Graham turned his tear-filled eyes towards him and nodded his head. 'Is she going to be all right?'

'There is nothing more we can do except wait. At least we know who she is now.'

Outside the cubicle the doctor led him away with a comforting arm around his shoulder, assuring him that everything possible would be done to get her well again.

'About my Mum,' Graham asked. 'Where is she?'

'Can't help you there I'm afraid, you see in emergencies of this nature and scale, ambulances are brought in from the surrounding area available, in this case they came from Retford and Worksop. It was easy to identify your father because of the contents in his wallet, but in the case of women involved in an accident the paramedics are concerned in getting the injured to hospital as quickly as possible; and in many cases items like handbags and their owners get parted.'

Still with his arm around Graham's shoulder the doctor stopped at a row of chairs alongside a wall. 'Sit there a moment, I'll make a phone call.'

Graham sat on one of the chairs, inwardly praying that Zoe would be all right.

Nurses were busy moving around him, young doctors passed him carrying clip-boards, the telephone at a nearby desk never seemed to stop ringing. A nurse pushing a drugs trolley passed by giving Graham a smile as she passed. Five minutes passed, the doctor re-appeared and sat down beside him.

'This has been a very trying time for you and you show great courage.' The doctor took a handkerchief from his pocket and blew his nose.

'This was a terrible accident in atrocious conditions, lots of people got injured and three were killed outright. He put his hand on Graham's shoulder and looked at him. 'I want you to come to the mortuary with me for identification.'

'Oh GOD!' exclaimed Graham, 'NO, not Mum . . . please . . .'

'We don't know yet. This way.'

Leaving the warmth of the building and stepping out into the cool air they walked across a paved area lined with potted plants and a long flowerbed running down the centre. A pale sun was trying to shine, breaking through large areas of cumulus cloud after the torrential rain of the previous day. Large pools of water still lay on the coloured tiled floor making them zig-zag their walk to avoid them as they headed for a red brick building with a green painted door. Neither spoke. The doctor rang the bell.

A small flap in the door opened revealing the heavily lined face of a bald man wearing thick pebble lens spectacles. The doctor explained the purpose of the visit and the door was opened for them. The temperature dropped suddenly as they stepped into a well lit room devoid of all colour. The whole room was painted white with white tiles on all walls from floor to ceiling. There was a row of cupboards along one side of the room and a very large stainless steel sink with three taps, one with a hosepipe fixed to it. A series of hand towels hung on a rack close by. In the centre of the room stood a large oversized adjustable table with drainage gullies and a waste pipe fixed at the far end of it disappearing into the floor. Above the table hung a large moveable electric lamp. The small of disinfectant and formaldehyde wrapped itself around Graham – he felt sick.

Dr Wainwright looked hard at Graham with a weak smile. Patting him on the arm, he suggested he sit down while he went into another room leading off.

135

Graham looked about him as he was left alone in a cold uninviting room. Eventually Dr Wainwright re-entered the room and beckoned Graham to follow him. As they entered a smaller room water still lay on the floor, it was cold and the smell of disinfectant followed him. He shuddered slightly when he saw a table in the centre covered completely with a white cloth almost touching the floor.

'Are you ready for this?' The question was shot at him like an arrow.

Graham nodded his head slowly and was directed to the side of the table. Dr Wainwright and the other white coated man stood either side of him as a third assistant moved to the end of the table and slowly pulled back the white cover revealing the face of Gemma – his mother.

'Mum!' He cried. 'NO, no, no . . .'

'All right, lad,' said the assistant, putting the sheet back in place. 'She would have died instantly – her neck was broken on the initial impact, in fact she would be dead before they hit the central reservation barrier.'

Graham stood motionless, unable to move a muscle. Suddenly he felt alone. The full impact suddenly hit him like a blow from a heavyweight boxer's fist. His mother lay dead, his sister in a coma and his dad on traction with his leg broken in two places and a broken pelvis. Objects around him became blurred and out of focus. The light in the room dimmed, he began to sway and slowly he was engulfed in a black cloud, and finally his strength left him as he dropped in a heap on the cold floor.

Regaining consciousness sometime later he found himself in a room with a nurse looking after him.

'Hello,' she said as he made a movement.

'Where am I?' he asked. 'What happened?'

'You passed out, now you are in a hospital room.'

'My dad . . . I've got to tell my dad what I know.'

'By now Dr Wainwright will have told him. He went straight off when you identified your mother.'

SEVENTEEN

Gemma was cremated at Loughborough crematorium after a short service. Her name was entered in the book of remembrance.

No one was ever found responsible for the cows' escape.

Zoe had made a complete recovery and was back at work as a fully qualified hairdresser. Graham, still haunted by the image of his mother lying in the mortuary, was finding it difficult to adjust to everyday society again. Robert was now crippled for life, his right leg pinned together and his pelvis repaired. 'They did a fibre-glass job on my pelvis,' he told people. The loss of his wife Gemma had left him devastated. Wherever he went in the house he was constantly reminded of her. The grand piano standing silent in the room was sold as Zoe could not find it in herself to play it. The music of Chopin still lingered on throughout the house. Gemma's clothes still hung in her wardrobe. Her cosmetics adorned her dressing table. Her personal notepaper and envelopes in her writing desk still lingered with her perfume.

Her funeral was attended by her sister from South Africa, her mother from Chorley, Jackie Reynolds and her daughter Roslin, her former flat mate Helen and Gerald her husband with baby Monica, Grace her one time cleaner and baby sitter for many years, and villagers from nearby Rothley, all showing great respect in their final goodbyes.

Some ventured to ask Robert what he intended to do now. There could be no answer to that question – not yet. He needed time. One major decision had to be made: the frequent visits to London and travelling about had got to end. He would retire.

He blamed himself for Gemma's death – he should never have attempted to overtake that tanker in those conditions. He could not see clearly enough to manage the situation. We never can see clearly those we love, we are too close – too much a part of them. Like a fog he could not see through it. Time they say heals, but for Robert time no longer existed. He found himself in an empty void, alone and broken.

FOUR YEARS LATER

Dr Robert Watts limped along the water edge of an incoming tide with the aid of a walking stick. A small canvas bag around his shoulder and a small black and white Jack Russell dog in front of him named 'Sparky'. It was bitterly cold. The onshore north-easterly wind was whipping up the loose sand, stinging his face as he pushed himself against the invisible force. Sparky was running in front of him in ever increasing circles chasing seagulls each time they landed. Two fishermen stood beside their fishing rods wearing duffle coats, flapping their arms and stamping their feet in an effort to keep warm, and each gave Robert a nod as he passed. In the distance a jogger in a red tracksuit appeared with good rhythmic steps keeping an eye on Sparky as he drew nearer, but Sparky was much too busy eyeing up his next prey.

The castle on its rock of dolerite loomed in the distance as he turned away from the sea into the sheltered area towards the ruined priory away from the constant wind. The noise of the pounding sea lessened the further he walked on. The stone walls of the old priory and rainbow arch stood stark against the cumulus-filled sky. With no more gulls to chase Sparky settled down to a more sedate walk beside Robert. Passing the statue of Saint Aidan and the railed off tomb of Grace Darling he entered the road of cottages leading to his sanctuary 'Sea Winds'.

Sparky was curled up in his basket feeling exhausted after his energetic encounter with the gulls on the beach. Robert filled the kettle in the kitchen for a cup of tea then sat back in the easy chair. He had returned to his cottage on Lindisfarne four weeks ago, bracing himself against the reminders of happier days and the last time he was here with Gemma and Zoe, a visit which ended in tragedy. In some way he felt safe here, away from the bustling outside world, the memory of his parents ever present within the fabric of the walls, his mother Mary in the kitchen, his father smoking his pipe and reading the newspaper, and his room upstairs still displaying his 'Finds'.

It was here he escaped from London when Linda lost her life in the Chinese earthquake shortly before they were due to marry, long before he met Gemma ... The cottage 'Sea Winds' had always offered shelter and protection for him. This was his home, his roots. Now he recalled the last time he was here with Gemma, he could visualise her now sitting in the car waiting for him to lock up the cottage and collect Zoe on that atrocious wet-ridden morning. He lay back in the chair and closed his eyes, sinking into oblivion.

Four years had passed since that terrible accident, leaving him crippled, bringing his working life to an abrupt end. His home in Charnwood Forest seemed empty without Gemma. Zoe and Graham were out all day working, leaving him alone with his thoughts, so a decision was made after consultation. Graham would be given enough money to buy a new bungalow on the outskirts of Loughborough to be near to his work after his marriage. Zoe could buy a half-share with Tanya in the hairdressing salon in Berwick, sharing the flat above. He would return to the cottage on the island where it all began. Both could have their pick of the furniture from their old home.

How long he had been asleep in the chair he did not know but it was well past midday when he opened his eyes with the cup of tea by his side now cold. Stretching himself he got up and walked down the garden path, followed by Sparky. The wind had dropped. The air around was still, as if in slack tide. The noise of the traffic and movement of vehicles suggested the tide was down and the pulse of the island had quickened. He stood looking at the delapidated wooden boat of his father. On the sea he could see the sails of small yachts sliding along majestically. Long wreaths of mist hung like a white veil in the far distance. He took in large gulps of fresh air. He felt very lonely, with no member of his family near or around him. Life for him now was desperately unhappy.

Sparky yapped, making him look around him.

'Hi!' came a voice from the direction of the gate. Turning round towards it, his heart missed a few beats. Jackie stood there, looking as beautiful as ever, dressed in stylish beige slacks with a high necked pale blue jumper.

He limped towards her. 'Hello Jackie!' He started, 'How did you ... ?'

'I had my hair done the other day. Zoe is my new hairdresser now, she told me you had sold up and were back in your cottage on the island. Thought I would come and see for myself. Hope you don't mind?'

'Of course not, it is a pleasant surprise. Let us go inside.'

The sight of her sitting before him looking like a fashion model from the pages of *Vogue* lifted his spirits. He found himself speechless. It was Jackie who opened the conversation. 'It is good to see you getting about. I have often thought of you, wondering how you were coping, so when Zoe told me you were now living on the island, I just had to come and see you.'

'Jackie, you are like a tonic. I have been so low, it seems that all I have worked for has been for nothing, taken away from me. I am back where I started all those years ago, in my cottage, by the sea, on my own. How is that for progress?'

'So what happens now, what do you want to do?'

'Well I'm sixty now, I have lost my wife, my two kids are now set up and I have been left crippled – what is there left?'

'Robert, I am fifty-nine, I have spent most of my so called married life on my own. I have not seen my husband for over three years now, but I am not ready to call it a day yet.' She stopped to take out a handkerchief from her handbag. 'I had a letter from him two weeks ago asking me for a divorce. I have always had my suspicions, now he tells me he has been living with his secretary for two years. The only good thing is, he has kept things going until Roslin left home. He wants me to put the house on the market after I have had it valued. He has not the guts to come and discuss it with me. He says I can have half the proceeds. How is that for twenty-four years of married life? I have lost a life.'

Silence fell about the room like a black cloud. Robert sat looking at the ceiling then down towards her, detecting tears rolling down her cheeks.

'At least, Robert, you had a life together – I never had one,' she sobbed.

Robert changed the subject. 'Would you like a drink?' he asked.

She nodded her head in reply, touching his hand as he rose from the chair.

'Perhaps you would like to walk to the harbour with me and Sparky afterwards.'

She smiled. 'That would be nice.'

Sparky ran in front of them, delighted to be out rummaging in the tall grass. Robert limped along slowly with Jackie by his side. How different it all was now. Robert a free man again, Jackie about to divorce, walking side by side almost like strangers, keeping apart. 'Remember the last time we walked down here?' he asked.

140

'Yes,' she answered, 'I remember many things we did, we had good times together.'

Along the quayside men in yellow oil-skin jackets were busy unloading boxes of crabs and fish, and the noise and smell of fish filled the air as they approached closer.

There was no longer a Jack Mason, he had retired two years ago and was now living near Newcastle to be near his son. Snowy White the sheep farmer had died of cancer a year ago. In fact the whole group had changed, it was a new generation of fishermen, things had altered drastically over the past three or four years. Life was changing before them in every respect. Robert turned to go back as Sparky was getting too near the men working on the quay. Jackie drew herself nearer to him and put her arm through his. He responded by covering her hand with his. She smiled at him.

Back at the cottage she sat on the settee while Robert prepared a meal for Sparky in the kitchen. Afterwards he cut sandwiches and re-entered with them on a tray.

'Robert you shouldn't,' she said, taking the tray from him.

Opening a cupboard door by the side of the fireplace and producing a black wooden box from it he withdrew a small stone. 'This,' he said, 'was picked up by Gemma on this beach the day I proposed to her. It is amber, some thirty to forty million years old. If you look at it closely you can see an insect trapped inside it. Gemma always said it was her lucky stone . . . I had forgotten about it until after she died . . . I would like you to have it Jackie.' He handed the box to her.

'Oh Robert, it is lovely, but I think you should keep it as a reminder.'

'I don't need it to remind me, I have two children and many memories, besides she said it was her lucky stone, perhaps it will bring you some luck.'

'That poor creature trapped all that time, a bit like me in a way.' She half smiled. 'Perhaps it will bring me some luck. Thank you, I shall treasure it.'

A whiff of her perfume reached him, making him want to hold her in his arms like he did years ago . . . but he froze, the memory of Gemma still haunting him and the way in which she died through his own stupidity that fateful day. Jackie too was in a dilemma, uncertain how to answer her husband's letter seeking a divorce. Where would it leave her. Was there a turning point?

* * *

He returned to the cottage after Jackie left, having watched her car draw away until it was a mere speck in the distance. Sparky jumped onto his knee as he sat down. He sank back in the chair stroking the dog, deep in thought. When the accident happened with the loss of Gemma, everything stopped. He was engulfed and thrown into the dark side of life. HE had died even though his body still lived. It did not seem possible that one could go on. Then through the swirling mist in his mind, beautiful Jackie had reappeared, once more distraught and lonely with her life falling apart around her.

He sat there with his faithful companion on his knee until it grew dark.

The following morning he was up and dressed early. Sparky was delighted to be out early chasing seagulls on the beach as they landed. The tide had turned but it would be some time before it was possible to cross onto the mainland. It was a warm morning in contrast to the previous day, a few streaks of white cloud and a rising sun with little chance of rain was a perfect start to his next assignment.

As the time for low tide approached he began to feel apprehensive and nervous, but his mind was made up. He was going to throw a lifeline.

Robert found himself splashing through the seawater pools left behind by the tide. Half-an-hour later he was mounting the three steps leading up Jackie's front door and ringing the bell.

'Robert!' she exclaimed in surprise, 'how nice to see you. What brings you here?'

'I'll soon know,' he said, brushing past her and entering the lounge.

'What's wrong?'

He paced up and down, then stopped at the window looking out. 'Jackie,' he started, 'life has given us both a severe blow. We have known each other almost a lifetime, therefore we are not strangers. In a way we are both trapped like that creature in that piece of amber. I loved you once, it hurt. I think I always have.

'Your husband wants a divorce, for the life of me I don't know why. Give it to him: release yourself from him Jackie. I am asking you to come and live with me, even marriage if you like. I'll have the place modernised to your liking. Let us be happy together. We could even buy a place in Berwick, a small flat where we could live during the winter months and visit the cinemas and concerts, with places to eat in the evenings.' Silence followed. He stood looking out of the window, memories flooded back to him. It was here he first met Gemma at the garden party. It was here in the room upstairs he first made love to Jackie. His heart began to pound waiting for her answer. Jackie rose from her chair and stood close behind him. He could feel her presence. He wanted to speak, ask her for an answer, but he froze. Then she broke the long silence. 'Robert darling, you won't see the sea from this window, but you can from our windows in the cottage.'

He swung round. 'Jackie!' he cried, tears rolling down his cheeks, 'You mean . . .? Oh darling, I love you so much.'

'Yes – I love you too – always have,' she answered, throwing her arms around him. 'I'm so happy . . .'